The Sacred Door and Other Stories

This series of publications on Africa, Latin America, Southeast Asia, and Global and Comparative Studies is designed to present significant research, translation, and opinion to area specialists and to a wide community of persons interested in world affairs. The editor seeks manuscripts of quality on any subject and can usually make a decision regarding publication within three months of receipt of the original work. Production methods generally permit a work to appear within one year of acceptance. The editor works closely with authors to produce a high-quality book. The series appears in a paperback format and is distributed worldwide. For more information, contact the executive editor at Ohio University Press, 19 Circle Drive, The Ridges, Athens, Ohio 45701.

The Ohio University Research in International Studies series is published for the Center for International Studies by Ohio University Press. The views expressed in individual volumes are those of the authors and should not be considered to represent the policies or beliefs of the Center for International Studies, Ohio University Press, or Ohio University.

The Sacred Door and Other Stories

Cameroon Folktales of the Beba

Makuchi

Foreword by Isidore Okpewho

Ohio University Research in International Studies
Africa Series No. 86
Ohio University Press
Athens

Printed in the United States of America

16 15 14 13 12 11 10 5 4 3 2

The books in the Ohio University Research in International Studies Series
are printed on acid-free paper ∞ ™

Library of Congress Cataloging-in-Publication Data

Makuchi, 1958–
The sacred door and other stories : Cameroon folktales of the Beba / Makuchi ; foreword by Isidore Okpewho.
p. cm. — (Ohio University research in international studies, Africa series ; no. 86)
The author retells the stories she heard while growing up in her native Cameroon.
Includes bibliographical references.
ISBN-13: 978-0-89680-256-8 (pbk. : alk. paper)
ISBN-10: 0-89680-256-6 (pbk. : alk. paper)
1. Tales—Cameroon. I. Title.
PR9372.9.M34S33 2008
398.2326711—dc22

2007035121

For Nfah Sulpitius Ndeh

April 20, 1961–January 24, 1999

Contents

Foreword, ix
Preface, xvii

Part 1

The Story of Bat and Sun, 3
The Story of Hawk and Hen, 5
The Story of Pig and Tortoise, 8
The Story of Cat and Rat, 12
The Story of the Birds That Went to the Sky, 15
The Story of Cat and Dog, 20
The Story of Monkey and Bee, 24
The Foolish Leopard, 27
Tiger Kills His Mother, 34
A Tug-of-War, 41
The Race, 45

Part 2

Metse-Tsate-Nfo, aka Sense-Pass-King, 53
The Man-Eating Lion, 59
The Flutes, 63

The Boy and the Dish, 71
The Unhappy Stepson, 76
The Disobedient Son, 80
The Two Sisters, 83
The Girls Who Refused Suitors, 96
Mbaka and the Magic Ring, 107
The Dance in the Sky, 111
The Quest, 116
Union Is Strength, 126

Part 3

Penis, Testicles, and Vagina, 131
When You Eat Today, Remember There Is Tomorrow, 134
The Greedy Mother, 137
The Ring and the String of Beads, 140
The Huntress, 145
King-of-Scabies, 150
Pumpkin, Pumpkin, Back to the Stem, 158
A Secret Is Difficult to Keep, 164
The Test, 167
The Sacred Door, 170
Hunting Elephants, 173

Afterword, 177

Foreword

Makuchi is right in observing, in her preface, the "dearth of Cameroon oral narrative collections in English." The phenomenon is not limited to Cameroon, and there are two possible reasons for it. The first is the sad decline in intensive scholarly research in African oral literature, especially on the continent itself. From the 1960s to the late 1980s, African scholars took on the challenge of exploring the oral traditions of their communities with a greater commitment and empathy than the European scholars who had earlier worked the same field. But with the collapse of structures sustaining honest endeavor in academic and other areas of life in African societies, many of these African scholars have emigrated to Western nations where their labors have found stable support. African scholars who have not migrated have been so embroiled in the struggle to survive the double jeopardy of depressed economies and philistine leadership that there is very little spirit—not to mention the needed resources—for sustained research.

The second is that the task of transcribing and translating oral narratives (and other kinds of oral art) has been rendered rather challenging by the ethnopoetic revolution of the 1970s, which has demanded of scholars a considerable faith in their representation of texts they collect from informants and artists, in such a way as to respect the orality of the enterprise and thus the accuracy of the material. The tales in Makuchi's collection are, by her account, from research she did between 1979 and 1987. Since leaving her country in 1988 for Canada and later the United States, she has had little opportunity to revisit the sources of her material to *re*-cognize the context that enabled the tales and to check them with the relevant personnel, many of whom may have passed away.

Still, Makuchi deserves to be commended for what she has offered us in this tale collection. For a start, the spirit behind the effort is admirable. The tales would be most valuable not only to African youths in the mother continent but especially to those in the new African diaspora in the Anglophone Western world. Because the tales are presented in a language and format that appeals more directly to a younger readership than in a frame specifically geared toward scholarly study, they would be particularly useful for bringing the lessons of the old traditions home to the appreciation of these youths.

The images and values contained in the tales reveal a characteristically tropical African environment and outlook. Tortoise, pig, monkey, and even the man-eating lion are as familiar to the tropical African world as co-wives in a polygamous household; so are the lessons of conduct they—animals and humans—yield us from their interactions. Of course, a good number of these tales offer naturalistic rationalizations of present-day phenomena intended, as these traditions have always been, to train the mind of the youth in the ways of inquiry and explanation; we should remember that in a traditional setting many of these tales were told by adults (mothers, uncles, and aunts) to youthful family members gathered in the yard, after supper, for lighthearted entertainment. So we have tales here like "The Story of Cat and Dog" and "The Story of Cat and Rat" that reflect on the antagonisms between animals that presumably lived happily together at the dawn of things. But even in the process, several of the tales offer moral and other lessons. For instance, in "The Flutes" we see how competitive envy in the polygamous home causes grief; in "The Unhappy Stepson" we find that, however much a child is repressed or marginalized, nothing will stop him/her from winning the success he/she is entitled to; in "The Disobedient Son," the future is bleak for a child who pursues a misguided path of stubbornness and recalcitrance; in "The Girls Who Refused Suitors," the fate of nubile girls who reject family counsel in favor of ill-advised individualism will be familiar to anyone who has read Amos Tutuola's *Palm-Wine Drinkard.* And so on.

Tales like these need to be retold again and again, because the lessons they yield belong not merely to a long-forgotten historical or so-called primitive past but very much to the present times in which we live. However far we think technological progress has taken us from the conditions in which our ancestors lived, we are still grappling with problems of personal conduct and of human relationships they faced in their day, though the cultural integers have changed somewhat. I particularly applaud Makuchi's restating the mores of African societies in the present tense, as a way of stressing that in whatever conditions we live today, the ideas that have guided our lives continue to be valid. "Our people measure wealth," she says in introducing the story "The Girls Who Refused Suitors," "not by the property one owns but by the members of one's family."

This leads me to what Makuchi says in her preface about part of the inspiration behind her recreating these tales. While she lived in Cameroon, she was well grounded in the tradition of participating in storytelling performances with members of her immediate and extended families, a practice she bid good-bye to upon relocating to North America. In southern Mississippi, however, she found an opportunity to revisit that tradition when she was invited "to share my knowledge of African traditions and cultures" with students in the area's middle and high schools, who brimmed with excitement at participating in the telling of stories, and the riddles that usually precede them, in traditional African performance situations.

I was struck by Makuchi's record of these encounters because I had a similar experience of telling African folktales to youngsters in the Binghamton school district recently, during a Martin Luther King Jr. memorial day program. There is no doubt that American children, black and non-black, are excited by stories from foreign traditions, and can be easily coaxed to provide a level of enthusiastic participation that African children back home readily offer. But these folk traditions are beginning to enjoy a significant resurgence even with more discerning adults. A graduate student in my own university recently approached me to discuss my work in oral literature, about which he happened to have learned. It turned out he was in biological sciences, but had considerable interest in folk traditions. He thought modern scientific education was all the poorer for its limited contact with the humanities and, in the course of our discussion, was amazed to find similarities between certain theories in folklore study and those that had been standard fare in scientific research. He revealed that there are efforts to reconnect the two fields of endeavor (the humanities and sciences), and would like me to come on his radio show for a discussion along these lines. Needless to say, I am looking forward to it.

I recall this event because I think that, although Makuchi has rightly targeted this collection of Cameroon folktales primarily, though not solely, at younger readers, I think it is a work that should appeal even to more mature audiences. The story of "Penis, Testicles, and Vagina" certainly lends itself more to adult interest, for obvious reasons, although any African who grew up in a traditional village should be honest enough to admit we performed a lot of sexual folklore out of the hearing of our parents (who were not unaware of some of the things we did to amuse ourselves)! But Makuchi's collection is clearly welcome material even for scholarly reflection, especially in terms of symbolic and other forms of analysis.

Let's face it: Is it really true that some of these animal tales were intended simply to amuse little children or even tickle their creative and/or rational intelligence? Is it not possible that the tales were imaginative disguises for critical comments on the conduct of certain powerful figures in traditional society, whose real names and personalities the oral artists were afraid to expose to easy recognition? I am suggesting it's time we mined our so-called folktales for the same level of serious insight that historians have, for the last four decades at least, found in oral testimonies. We need to do this, because we owe it to ourselves to probe the roots of our contemporary social and political malaise—if I may recall a counsel from Chinua Achebe, to find out "where the rain began to beat us"—so as to disabuse ourselves of them. Our study of oral literature cannot be excused from the sorts of hard questions other intellectual disciplines have been asking for some time.

Makuchi is right, of course, in stressing that the tales in this collection have the primary goal to delight and to teach the youth of today, whether they live in Africa or in the diaspora. While she recognizes that she is presenting these tales outside the format of storytelling performance in the traditional context, she retains enough consciousness of that context to instill it in some of the tales here. It was important for her to remind us, as she does in her preface, that storytelling was "and continues to be a communal experience" in her African homeland, so as to prepare us for the atmosphere of collective representation that she conjures in the tales. The live interactive voice of the narrator strikingly prefaces the story titled "The Flutes," which conjures a circle of children gathered in the moonlit yard for a narrative session with a mother or an aunt, as well as the convivial atmosphere in which Makuchi's family "ate food, drank mostly palm wine and sometimes beer, socialized, and told *ble* [tales]." In "The Story of Hawk and Hen," which narrates the involvement of the Cockroach in a crisis facing this family of fowls, the narrator foreshadows the tragic fate of an interaction between predator (Hen) and prey (Cockroach) by pointedly drawing the audience's attention: "Was this a big mistake? I don't know." And in "The Story of the Birds That Went to the Sky," which clearly recalls a similar tale in Achebe's *Things Fall Apart,* the narrator repeatedly demands her audience's attention to her efforts with the phrase "I tell [*or,* am telling] you." For good measure, in true Achebe-esque fashion, the didactic or proverbial wisdom of the tales is emphasized, as at the start of "The Story of Cat and Dog."

Makuchi pointedly stresses this didactic mission in a whole paragraph prefacing the tale of "The Girls Who Refused Suitors," where she makes a careful point about traditional African expectations of the institutions of marriage. At any rate, there are so many tales dealing with—and carefully elucidating in gnomic and other diction—the moral lessons to be learned from various dramas of relationship, that it is clear Makuchi has designed this collection primarily as a tool for inculcating knowledge of elements of African culture and only secondarily as pleasurable reading. And she is just as interested in presenting these lessons to a general as well as a parochial African audience. Living and interacting with black and other races in North America has brought home to her the need to tease out the larger humane virtues from the African world in language and style that would appeal to a diverse readership. Who would not recognize the harm that results from disloyalty between friends or unkindness to a stepchild, even when these are framed by images and symbols from a foreign culture? The story of "The Sacred Door" teasingly recalls the injunction on Adam and Eve, or even Lot's wife, though the consequences of failure are not as dire as in either of the biblical tales. But the question the narrator poses about the behavior of the poor farmer in this brilliant dilemma tale—"What would you have done?"—would, without question, appeal as much to a Chinese or Scottish as to an African ethical consideration.

Makuchi may lament, as she does in her preface, that leaving her native Beba home in Cameroon has removed her from the warm, familial environment in which the tales in her collection were originally told, or that she has not succeeded in recreating with her children the traditional context of cultural education in which she was raised. But she is bringing that education to a larger, universal audience that includes her own children here in North America who, in time, will come to recognize that—to paraphrase an old Igbo (Nigerian) proverb—"Where you mend the roof, there is your home."

Isidore Okpewho
Binghamton University

Preface

Storytelling was a fact of life, intrinsic to my early upbringing in Cameroon. I heard stories about my country, but I also learned about my people, the Beba.[1] Because my father was a teacher, we traveled a lot when I was a child. We moved to Beba for the first time when I was twelve, already a secondary school student. My earliest and strongest memories of storytelling sessions date back to my parents' "return to the native land"—as older relatives were wont to remind us, the children. It was a common occurrence in our household to share oral narratives, what the Beba call *ble*, and commonly referred to as folktales, in the evenings when we came home from school or the farms where we plowed the land and planted, tended, and harvested most of our food crops.[2] My mother was always the one to initiate storytelling sessions, either while we sat down around the evening fire waiting for food to cook or after we had finished eating. My father rarely initiated these sessions, though we knew that as a schoolteacher, he scheduled storytelling sessions in his lesson plans. *Ble* were not and still are not told during the daytime except of course to accommodate modern demands. An exception can be made for daytime storytelling in school during the class period known as "Story Time." Young Beba children are often told that *bekwu* will steal their voices if they indulge in storytelling during the daytime. Older children who know the "truth" and understand the reasons behind this injunction use it as a weapon to taunt and frighten their younger siblings. The young ones learn as they grow up that ghosts do not in fact usurp their voices so long as they understand the purpose of reserving storytelling for those evening hours when families gather and take stock of that day, the days before, and those to come; in short, when they sit down to take stock of their lives. I grew up in a family of ten children comprising seven brothers and three sisters.[3] My extended family of cousins, aunts, uncles, grandfathers, grandmothers, nieces, and nephews make for a much larger kinship. Storytelling was then and continues to be a communal experience.

I left that communal experience behind when I moved to North America in the late 1980s, but I "reconnected" with telling *ble* while living in Hattiesburg and teaching at the University of Southern Mississippi. I had the opportunity of meeting with students in southern Mississippi's middle and high schools. I also met with youths participating in after-school programs run by community centers. I was invited to share my knowledge of African traditions and cultures with the young people. I met with teachers and educators interested in African oral narratives and storytelling; in making connections between African traditions and the American or African American diasporic experience. My conversations on oral traditions with the students always began with the *le-nkwang*, or call-response, warm-up chatter typical of the Beba riddle sessions.[4] Children are the main participants in riddle sessions; adults listening on the sidelines only chime in to assist them with answers to their queries. Riddle sessions test children's wit and their knowledge of their people, customs, culture, and environment. I therefore told the students riddles and encouraged them to locate possible answers in their own American or immediate cultural contexts or environment. I would give them the Beba answers to the riddles only after they had struggled to come up with their own. Next, I would ask them to pose their own riddles. Quite often, the children were at a loss. Some would bluntly tell me that they watched television instead of telling stories or learning riddles. But I would give them popular (American) examples such as "I am black and white and read all over"; "What travels around the world but never leaves the corner?" Once they recognized these riddles, the connection made it easier for some to come up with their own, either familiar or new.

Following the riddle sessions, I would tell the students some *ble*. We would then engage in a general discussion, group exercises, or both. I would end these conversations by answering the many questions they always had about Africa: Where is your grass skirt? How do you get up the trees? Those discs you wear in your ears—don't they hurt? Did you learn to wear shoes in America? How often did you play with lions? Can you please dance and jump really high for us? Do y'all have schools over there in Africa? These questions often revealed what they "know" about "Africa" from hearsay, from watching the Learning Channel, National Geographic, or American popular culture about Africans on other television network programming. (Incidentally, this is not unique to middle and high school students. When colleagues or other college professors in such fields as world literature and world civilizations invited me to meet with their classes, some college students asked questions in the same vein.) The students' innocent, sometimes ignorant questions notwithstanding, the one thing I took away from these exchanges was the students' enthusiasm, for once they fully engaged with the riddles and tales, we stopped only reluctantly because of time constraints. The teachers and college professors I met in schools consistently talked of the need to teach or read oral narratives with their students, and the parents I interacted with in after-school programs expressed the desire to read folktales with or to their children. I had been doing at these schools some of what Isidore Okpewho has described as "cultural education." He asks:

> How is it possible for the citizens of a society to acquire, on a general or collective basis, information concerning themselves: who they are, their origins and connections, and the peculiar ways of living and behaving that identify them as a people and that must be preserved for the sake of cultural continuity? Obviously, such information is contained in the various forms of oral literature practiced in the society—songs, narratives, proverbs, riddles, and so on—which are delivered either privately (e.g., mother to child, artist to apprentice) or publicly (e.g., in moonlight entertainment or in open performances by skilled artists). Through these media the younger members of society absorb the ideas that must be kept alive for the benefit of those coming behind them. (*African Oral Literature*, 115)

Working with students, teachers, and parents in South Mississippi took me back to those childhood years. Further, I am a fiction writer; I was writing short stories at the time, and I liberally use what I learned from my mother's stories in my own writing. Most of the tales, songs, and proverbs that I use in my fiction are borrowed directly from stories my mother told (see for instance the title story in my short story collection, *Your Madness, Not Mine*). It had been more than twenty years since I had done graduate research in oral literature. I decided to take my work in South Mississippi one step further. I decided to retell some of the memorable stories of my childhood, to re-create those stories commonly told in my family—an experience shared not only by the immediate family but by all those who had visited on such evenings or who stood in the yard and bellowed the evening greeting, "*Neb nkwefo ko'uh?*" only to be wheedled into the kitchen or parlor by my mother's response, "*Why am I hearing a voice without seeing a face?*" The dearth of Cameroon oral narrative collections in English was an added incentive. Working on this book also had personal implications of enriching connections between my Beba/Cameroonian cultural identity and my daily life in the United States. This project made me realize how Beba riddles, and especially proverbs, were slowly fading from my daily discourse and communication with others. But as I recreated the narratives, the riddles and proverbs came with those memories. Being reimmersed in this worldview has therefore been both intimidating and invigorating.

After earning my BA in bilingual letters (English and French—Licence ès Lettres Bilingues) at the University of Yaounde, I chose the oral literature concentration for my graduate studies, from 1979 to 1987, in the Department of Negro-African Literature, then headed by Dr. Bernard Fonlon. Fieldwork took me to Beba, where I enjoyed *ble* or storytelling evenings as usual with family members. Even though I had heard the same stories for many years while I was a student in secondary and high school, I had never dreamed I would one day be doing research on those stories. We were too immersed in the Anglo-Saxon curriculum of O levels and A levels to give any value to this oral literature in school. However, in 1979 I had to record *ble* narrated by family members, some of which made up the primary source material for my thesis and later my dissertation.[5] One of the requirements oral literature students had to fulfill was to record, transcribe, and translate their material, all of which was presented as an appendix in their dissertation. (Many students shied away from graduate work in oral literature because of this requirement.) I therefore transcribed my family's tales in Beba, then provided a literal translation and a final literary translation in my dissertation.

That was more than two and a half decades ago. I have moved a lot since. Between 1981 and 1988 I moved five times within Cameroon: from Yaounde in the Central Province to Foumban in the West Province, from the West Province to three different locations (Fontem, Tiko, Limbe) in the South West Province and from there to Douala in the Littoral Province; then on to Montreal, Canada, in 1988 and the United States in 1994. In the process of packing, moving, and unpacking in Cameroon, property (including tape recordings, films of photographs, and exercise books with handwritten notes) was damaged, lost, sometimes even destroyed or discarded by relatives in whose homes it had been stored over the years. The oral narratives of my graduate work have therefore never been published. The folktales presented in this book are my recreation of some of those stories we shared as a family—before and after I did graduate work—while we ate food, drank mostly palm wine and sometimes beer, socialized, and told *ble*.

Although storytelling was a family affair back then, I owe a particular debt and tribute to my mother, who played the pivotal role of getting things started and keeping them going. Ever since her death in 1984, I can hardly remember us, her children, duplicating as a group the family tradition she started, nor have we done so with my stepmother (who is not Beba). Complicating this situation is the fact that as we got older and more Western-educated we moved away to other parts of the country, and even abroad, where we are raising our own families. Over the years our family visits to Beba have been infrequent. Sadly, we have not been following my mother's example with her grandchildren in our own homes, wherever we are. I see my retelling of these folktales as another link in the chain of that creative spirit and legacy and also as a mea culpa to my own children, who, I might add, speak very little Beba.

Notes

1. Beba is an agrarian society, without modern electricity, where the people farm the land and grow most of the food crops that feed their families all year round. The Beba people speak Beba—a language with no written alphabet—and their village is also known as Beba. In colonial times, Beba village was referred to in official documents as Babaji but the name was changed in postcolonial times to appropriately reflect the people who live there.

2. In his seminal work, *African Oral Literature: Backgrounds, Character, and Continuity* (Bloomington: Indiana University Press, 1992), Isidore Okpewho has noted, and rightly so, regarding the term *folktale:* "So long as we disabuse our minds of the sort of prejudice which earlier generations of scholars had about the concept of folk as 'uneducated' and therefore irrational and unimaginative dwellers of small communities, then there may be situations in which we can excuse the use of the term *folktale* for purposes of convenience. The term *oral narrative* is, however, preferred not only because it leaves little room for that prejudice but also because—perhaps like the term *oral literature*—it gives primary emphasis to the medium of expression of this form of art, which is mouth to mouth" (163). I use the term *folktales* for convenience only, as my usage throughout eschews the prejudice Okpewho warns against and carries the full weight of "oral narratives," which I employ interchangeably with "folktales." (See my detailed discussion of *ble,* storytelling among the Beba, and a brief history of Cameroon in the Afterword.) Similarly, I use the term *farm(s)* instead of *fields* because people in Cameroon more often than not speak of going to their farms rather than fields.

3. My mother died on August 15, 1984. Three of my brothers are also deceased: Nfah Ezekiel Takumberh died on December 26, 1995; Nfah Sulpitius Ndeh on January 24, 1999, and Nfah Jude Nkontemur on March 22, 2001. My father remarried, and our family grew to include a stepsister, a half brother, and a half sister, Josepha Nfah, who died on March 16, 1998.

4. *Le,* meaning "Lend me your ears" and *nkwang,* meaning "We are listening."

5. Those who narrated stories then ranged in age from eight to seventy-five: my brothers Sylvester Nsemelah, Eustace Mbaka, and Sulpitius Ndeh; my sister, Mary Baba; my mother, Patricia Ngonda; my uncles Fidelis Afuba and Leo Ajonjap; my cousins Mathias Awafe, Ayanga Abara, Mary Ngwebu, Justina Ngwebu, Justina Ngonda, and Bridget Flike; Justina Ngonda's brother-in-law, Martin Akowah; my uncle's wife, Veronica Mukwele; and Eustace Mbaka's schoolmates Roseline Njietoh and Prisca Manoji. Many other family members participated but did not tell stories.

Part 1

The Story of Bat and Sun

Once upon a time, Aleleb-the-Bat and Neneb-the-Sun had a good friendship, a friendship stronger than *ngwalii.* They were like finger and nail. It is said that they were such good friends they were always visiting one another. Sometimes, they'd spend one night at Bat's home and the next night at Sun's compound.

One day, Bat went to visit Sun. On this visit, they spent a few days together. And then Bat went home only to find his mother seriously ill. You remember the saying that the strongest tree is the one that sprouts from beneath a rock? Bat had always seen his mother as one such tree. She had taken care of him through good times and many hardships. Now Bat feared for his mother's life. He flew from the compound of one healer to another pleading for their help. The healers gave the ailing woman potent herbs. They poured libations and called on the ancestors to watch over Bat's mother. They did their outmost, but Bat's mother's health worsened alarmingly and she grew weaker and weaker with each passing day.

"My son, I can feel that my time has come to leave you and join the ancestors. Do not grieve after I am dead. You must continue to be dutiful and take good care of yourself," she said, her breathing coming in short gasps. "If I have taught you anything, it is this: the rain which beats on a stone merely washes its body. You have been a good son and I know you will find the strength to go on." Bat's mother spoke these words one evening to her son and died.

Bat was inconsolable. His grief-stricken heart was as heavy as the *ngwalii* stone. He knew what he had to do. He decided to honor his mother by burying her before darkness threw its shadow over the village. My friend can wait until I've buried my mother, he reasoned happily, and rushed to see Sun.

Bat said, "Sun, my ailing mother has died. Hold your light. Please let your light shine a little longer. Give me the time to bury Mother-of-Mine. You can put out your torch after I have finished laying her to rest."

"My good friend, I know you need me but I'm sorry that I can't wait for you to bury your mother," Sun replied. "Can't you wait for daybreak?"

"How can you ask me that? Death has snapped the shoulder bone on the spot where the bag is carried. What kind of a friend are you?" Bat moaned and flew off into the twilight.

Bat's throat grew bitter, more bitter than *ghee*.[1] "No, I must bury her today," the sobbing Bat kept repeating to himself. He arrived home as darkness fell and hurriedly buried his mother. It was completely dark by the time he was done. And so, in the deep of night, Bat lay down by his mother's grave and swore never to look upon Sun's face again. Never! He buried that friendship along with his mother. And that, it is said, is the reason why, from that day forward, bats have shunned the face of the sun and move about only at night.

The story is finished.

[1]A type of vegetable with a bitter taste; known in Pidgin English as bitter-leaf.

The Story of Hawk and Hen

There once lived two inseparable friends, Magheb-the-Hawk and Nguh-the-Hen. These two were likened to the hand and the head: neither sleeps without the other. Indeed, Hawk and Hen were known to go on trips together, sleep in the same bed, and eat from the same bowl. Hen had seven children and Hawk had four. Their children were always seen together on the playground.

One day, Hawk woke to find his oldest child running a fever. The child's skin had developed a rash of scabies. His body was hot all over and the child was in pain for several weeks. Hawk and Hen took turns cleaning the scabies and treating the wounds with palm oil, but all their efforts did not ease the child's pain. They wondered what else they could do. It so happened that Mbe-the-Cockroach was known throughout the land as a good and experienced doctor, so Hawk decided to go and ask for her help. Was this a big mistake? I do not know, but Hawk did not think twice about inviting this healer into his home. But it was known throughout the land that Cockroach and Hen hated each other, for wasn't it said that when Hen saw Cockroach all she saw was a plump juicy thing good only for her stomach? Hawk and Hen had been friends for so long that he was confident his friend would not betray his trust. He consoled himself with the thought that clouds do not always forecast rains but ignored the other saying that a leopard cub does not grow old before its spots are noticed. Throwing all caution to the wind, he went and pleaded with Cockroach, asking the healer to make the trip to his home. Cockroach said to Hawk, "Go back to your child. I'll be there as soon as I can." Hawk returned and waited and waited and waited. Cockroach finally arrived in the evening twilight, carrying a small bag containing a variety of herbs and the cure for Hawk's child. As you can imagine, the moment Hen set eyes on Cockroach she began to bat her wings and cluck around the compound in circles.

"Cockroach, you call yourself a healer? Are these the only herbs this child needs?" Hen immediately picked a quarrel when Cockroach crossed the threshold into Hawk's house. "Will these herbs heal Hawk's child? You haven't brought enough medicine because you want Hawk's child to die," Hen accused.

Cockroach ignored Hen. She sat on the chair Hawk offered her and removed the herbs from her bag. She spread them out on a plantain leaf in three piles. She spoke directly to Hawk.

"Soak this leaf, and this one, and this one in warm water every morning and evening," Cockroach instructed, pointing at each pile of herbs. "Use the infusion to bathe your child. After bathing the entire body, apply this *mero ngwob* to the wounds. The python's oil will heal the scabies and help the child sleep. I will bring the patient something to drink every evening before he goes to bed. Your child should be his old self in a week."

"I don't trust you," Hen interrupted. "Hawk should never have brought you here."

"Why haven't you treated the child yourself since you know our herbs so well?" Cockroach retorted. "Put some water on the fire," she barked at Hawk.

Hearing this rebuff, Hen flew into a rage. She was, as the Beba say, bitter-in-the-throat. She batted her wings even louder and proceeded to cluck-cluck cluck-cluck cluck-cluck around the *nsaa*.[1] She left the *nsaa*, but her clucking could be heard echoing in treetops. The more she flapped her wings, the more she clucked, the angrier she got. To everyone's surprise, she pounced on the plantain leaf and scratched it to pieces. The medicines went flying into the air. Hawk watched with consternation as everything suddenly went topsy-turvy. Cockroach paid no heed and went to work on the child. But Hen would not be ignored. She approached the healer and with one swift peck sunk her beak into Cockroach and swallowed her down with one loud gulp. There was no one else Hawk could turn to to treat his child. The child lived a few more hours and died. It was Hawk's turn to be bitter-in-the-throat. Hen should have remembered the saying that one does not defecate where one sleeps, for as the pepper suffers so too does the grinding stone. Hawk looked straight at Hen and swore, "The fate of the pot will also be that of the yam or my name isn't Hawk!" Without more ado he sought revenge by killing one of Hen's children. From that day, he made an oath: to kill any of Hen's children whenever and wherever their paths met. As you can imagine, the long-standing friendship between Hawk and Hen came to a painful end. And so the Beba say that is why hawks to this day hunt Hen's children.

The story is finished.

[1]A wide open space in a compound, located in front of a house (or houses) or between houses, where children play during the day and on moonlit nights, and where *ble* are sometimes told. The *nsaa* is also used to conduct ceremonies such as births, and for celebrations, such as deaths.

The Story of Pig and Tortoise

A long time ago, Ankwunyab-the-Pig was one of the wealthiest members of his community. He owned big farms from which he harvested and sold much of the crop. Rumor had it that Pig was such a successful farmer because he had a big appetite and so he diligently tended his crops. But Pig had a friend, Torokee-the-Tortoise, who was as lazy as Pig was hardworking. Tortoise's chronic laziness didn't thwart a lavish lifestyle; on the contrary. He was the opposite of his friend. Tortoise was as much a spendthrift as Pig was thrifty. He spent most of his life borrowing food and other household needs from his friend Pig.

One day, Tortoise asked his friend to lend him a considerable sum of money. "You still owe me the money I lent you last year to celebrate the birth of your child; you haven't returned the cocoyam seeds I lent you last planting season, or the calabash of palm oil, or the pots, or the cutlass, and here you are again asking me for so much money?" Pig moaned.

"My friend, my in-laws are coming for a visit. You know I need to give them a deserving welcome. I'd like you to be one of my honored guests."

Pig salivated at the thought of a big feast. He savored the idea of being an honored guest. Despite his misgivings he consented to give his friend the loan after all.

"You have one moon cycle to repay me," Pig pronounced, handing Tortoise half the amount he had requested.

"Thank you," Tortoise replied and went home to his wife.

One moon cycle came and went. Yet another passed. So did another and another and another, but Tortoise would not repay his debt. Pig made trips to Tortoise's home, but each time he returned empty-handed and irate, for he got virtually the same response from Tortoise: "Why are you bothering me so, oh Friend-of-Mine?" Tortoise protested. "I know I owe you the money . . . and all those other things you enumerate repeatedly. I know I'll pay you back. But how can I when you won't give me the time to harvest and sell my crops?"

Pig was not moved by Tortoise's display of pain. This year, while all the animals had gone far into the forest to plant their crops, Tortoise had farmed an area of sallow bushes close to his house. Everyone knew he was in for another poor harvest.

"Friend-of-Mine, don't forget that a person does not slaughter the hen which lays eggs just because there is a feast. You're behaving like the man who climbed up the tree of life and once there destroyed the ladder his kinsmen had made for that purpose. I'll come back in eight days. Make sure you have my money then," a seething, fed-up Pig warned. "If you don't produce that money you will for the first time see what I'm truly made of." Even so, Pig could not tell whether he was angrier at himself or this bone-lazy scallywag.

On the appointed day, Tortoise patiently awaited his friend's arrival. When he heard Pig grunting and huffing two compounds away, he lay on his back and asked his wife to use him as a grinding stone.

"Don't say a word to Pig when he comes here," Tortoise instructed his wife. "Make sure you go about your tasks as if he were not here. Ignore him no matter what he says," Tortoise reiterated and then pulled his head and legs into his shell.

Pig arrived at Tortoise's house and was welcomed by a sour-faced Mrs. Tortoise. She behaved exactly as her husband had directed. She concentrated on grinding her spices. She'd look up only to dip her fingers into a bowl of water. She'd sprinkle a few drops to moisten the spices. Gro gro gro gro went her small grinding stone.

"Are you deaf? Am I not talking to you?" Pig stammered. "I am asking you for the umpteenth time, where is your husband? He knew to expect me today. Where is he? I am wasting my time repeating myself, and you, all you do is grind your pepper? Won't you answer me? I say, where is your husband?" Pig grunted.

Mrs. Tortoise remained stubbornly mute. Completely exasperated and not knowing exactly what he was doing, Pig grabbed the stone and flung it violently into the plantain bush behind the house. Tortoise immediately stuck his head and limbs out, rose to his feet, shook the leaves off his shell, and strolled into his house a few minutes later. He feigned surprise at his weeping wife and glanced indifferently at the surly Pig.

Tortoise ignored Pig and addressed his wife: "Tegheh kwu! Dead-Father-of-Mine! Am I dead or are you praying for my death, Wife?"

Pig looked on, barely concealing his contempt.

"Mr. Pig came here and found me grinding spices for the soup I am cooking. He didn't even let me finish. He grabbed my grinding stone and . . . and threw it away and . . . and I haven't been able to finish cooking our evening meal," she sobbed.

"I had no intention of throwing away the stone," Pig cut in. "I asked her repeatedly where you were but she wouldn't dignify my request with an answer."

"Well, here I am. I am sorry my wife neglected to be a good hostess. I can assure you her mother taught her better manners. Please sit down. Tell me, what did you want?"

"I want my money," Pig said in a flat monotone. To Pig's surprise and exasperation, Tortoise gave his visitor a long look and guffawed as if Pig had just made the best joke he had ever heard.

"So, I am supposed to die of hunger because you want your money? My wife can't cook food in her own home because you want your money? Oh my! Here I was running home with your money. I've been running for the last hour because I wanted to get here with your money before you got here. I get here only to find you abusing my wife? My dear friend, I will overlook this insult this time. However, if you want your money back, you must first find my wife's grinding stone," Tortoise said with finality and walked over to his bed, leaving a dumbfounded Pig near the fireplace. Pig and Tortoise had been friends for so long he knew Tortoise was not bluffing. But how could he afford to lose fifty pounds because of a stupid stone? He went in search of that stone. His snout has been digging the earth since in the hopes of finding Mrs. Tortoise's grinding stone.

The story is finished.

The Story of Cat and Rat

This happened many many years ago. It was the year when the rains ravaged the landscape and floodwaters rotted the crops before they could be harvested. Famine and illness claimed many lives. Entire families were wiped out. Bushi-the-Cat and Mbia-the-Rat were among the lucky survivors. They became bosom friends. They pulled their meager resources together, lived in one house, ate from the same pot, and farmed their fields together. One day, they went to the market and bought some *mbwe tseb.* They cooked a delicious pot of soup with this mudfish; ate half of it, and saved the rest for the next day. They slept soundly and woke up relaxed and ready for work.

Cat took his cutlass, Rat his hoe and they set out for their farm four hills and three valleys away from the village. But while they trekked, Rat's thoughts kept meandering back to the *mbwe tseb.* He was unusually quiet and hardly exchanged words with Cat. Cat wondered about the absent-minded dazed look on Rat's face. They had barely traversed a valley and ascended and descended one hill when Rat threw his hoe down, tripped on the handle, fell to the earth, and grabbed his stomach.

"Oh my friend," he cried. "There's something wrong with me. I am seeing many skies. Everything is spinning around me."

"We probably ran down that hill too fast," Cat said. "Rest a while. If you feel better we'll stroll across this plain."

"I don't think it is the hill," Rat moaned.

Cat sat down, put Rat's head in his lap, and pressed his palm across Rat's brow.

"You're not well," Cat said, trying to help his friend up. "Come, let me take you home. I'll carry you on my back."

"No, my friend," Rat groaned rather quickly. "Why go to all that trouble? Don't worry. I'll walk slowly and I'll get home safely," Rat said, struggling to his feet.

"Well, if you're sure you can make it alone, then you can go, but I must at least go and inspect the farm before coming back to see how you're doing," Cat said, concerned for his friend.

Rat dragged his feet. You'd think he had an aching ankle, but as soon as Cat's back was out of sight, Rat flew, flew like a swallow, running as fast as he could to reach their house. When he got home, he made straight for the pot of mudfish. He impatiently knocked the lid off and, the gods forbid, he jumped straight into the pot! He ate and ate and ate until a tiny piece of fish lay lonely at the bottom of the pot. He thought of keeping that morsel for his friend, but his heart longed for it. His throat could not resist the temptation. He closed his eyes and finished off the last piece. Rat's stomach was so full it was as bloated as the belly of a child suffering from kwashiorkor. He tried to hop out of the pot but his stomach felt heavier with each jump. Many attempts later, Rat took a deep, long breath and made one final desperate effort. He landed on the mouth of the earthenware pot instead. The pot flipped upside down and locked him in. He remained trapped for the rest of the day.

Later that evening, Cat returned from their farm. To his surprise, Rat was not in bed. Maybe he's gone to ease himself, Cat thought. Cat waited for Rat to return, but when Rat did not show up he went to the small-house to look for him. Rat was not there. Cat walked round the compound. Rat was nowhere to be found. Worried, Cat returned to the house and continued his search from room to room. In the kitchen, he came upon the pot of mudfish. Its round bottom was in the air and the mouth was hugging the floor. "What could have happened here?" he wondered out loud. He bent down, stretched out his hands, and lifted the mouth of the pot. No sooner were his hands in the air than something shot past him and made directly for a hole. Ooh! Dead-Body-of-Mine, Cat cried. He was so startled that the pot fell from his hands and shattered to pieces. He swung around. He was just in time to catch a glimpse of the fleeing Rat.

"Ah, so that's why you told me you were ill. Liar! It's true that the anus of a fowl is seen only when the wind blows. You thief! You scoundrel! You are no friend of mine. When I catch you—and I will catch you—I'll eat you for your treachery," Cat bellowed, realizing how easily his friend had duped him. He was bitter-in-the-throat indeed. And so the Beba say that from that day, cats began to eat rats. Cats will hunt rats anytime and anywhere until their last breath.

The story is finished.

The Story of the Birds That Went to the Sky

Once every year, in a far-off land, all the birds went to the sky to mark the end of the harvest season. This important celebration also marked the end of one year and the beginning of another. It marked the period of rest that stretched lazily from the end of the harvest to the beginning of the next farming season. At the feast, the birds enjoyed a rowdy celebration, guttling mounds of food and guzzling kegs of wine until they were exhausted from merriment.

The year of our story, Torokee-the-Tortoise decided to accompany the birds to the skies. He had lived with the birds for thousands of years and many were his friends. He had never asked to accompany them before and was certain they could not refuse him an invitation. He made his intentions known to one of his closest friends, Magheb-the-Hawk.

"Ha ha ha! But you have no wings," Hawk guffawed, flapping his wings in Tortoise's face. "How on this earth of our ancestors do you intend to fly without feathers? I know you are quite the trickster, capable of doing anything you put your mind to—after all, you won a race against Hare, the fastest animal in the land. You made a fool of the largest animal in our forests. I don't know how Elephant sleeps at night after that tug-of-war. You not only convinced Tiger to kill his mother, you went as far as killing him yourself. You outsmarted and turned the wealthy Pig into a pathetic, grunting sight, digging the earth for the rest of his life. I know all that, but this . . . ?"

"My friend, our people say that if you follow the king's train you will eat the head of a chicken. I will have wings. I will borrow feathers from all the birds."

Hawk looked at his friend, suppressed a chuckle, shook his head, and flew away. Tortoise watched Hawk go, chuckling along with him, but promptly proceeded to go from home to home, friend to friend, nest to nest, persuading each and every one of the birds to give him a feather. He collected quite a pile. He took the bundle home. Using *nleh*, Tortoise's wife glued the assortment of feathers all over his smooth shell. He now had a pair of flappable wings. You could hardly see his little head sticking through the bouquet. I tell you, Tortoise looked so regal that some of the birds were openly jealous of the beautiful patterns their feathers had fashioned for him. But they soon forgot about Tortoise while they anxiously prepared for the feast. At last, they woke to the day of their departure and all the birds assembled at *gbweshi*, the place of gathering. Mashii'yeh-the-Parrot made a quick head count.[1] All the birds had arrived on time. Before Parrot could announce it was time for them to begin their long journey, Tortoise cleared his throat.

"Did you swallow a toad for breakfast?" Parrot teased, to boisterous laughter.

"Now that you mention it, I wish I had," Tortoise joked back. "This is what I wanted to say. I propose we change our names."

"Why?" Toor inquired, his tone baleful. Sunbird was one who never trusted Tortoise and worse, envied him his celebrated cunning.

"That's an element of surprise that will intrigue and impress our hosts. Let's choose names they've never heard of. They'll

[1]*Mashii* is a generic term meaning bird; *yeh* means talk, noise; hence, bird-of-talk, bird-that-talks; also, bird-of-noise.

wonder why they've never given such names to their own children. I'm certain our hosts will see this as innovative," Tortoise replied with his usual poise.

Some birds protested and refused to change their names but others agreed it was a good idea; some saw it as a playful ploy nonetheless. Weren't they after all going to the sky to enjoy themselves? Nchanewe, the keeper-of-time, the early riser who enjoys the sweet smell of waking buds, quickly chose the name Flower. Ghane-the-Swallow followed Clockbird, choosing the name Arrow. Mashii'nki, the sleek waterbird known as Kingfisher, baffled them all with the name Long-Throat even though he was known to possess a healthy appetite. Tortoise quietly said, "My name is All-of-You." Some of the birds laughed, some looked nervous, some scoffed, berating him for such a superfluous name, while others simply shrugged it away. When all the birds so inclined had chosen a new name, they took off happily for the skies.

Their hosts warmly welcomed this gregarious group of guests and offered them comfortable seats. "Have you arrived?" they greeted. "Welcome, welcome," they enthused. "How was your journey? Are your relatives at home in good health? How was the harvest this year? No clouds on your tail as you flew here, we hope." The guests joined in the cheer and the chitchat. While the guests responded to questions about their families, one group of hosts showed them to their seats; another hauled out basins loaded with Antaean proportions of assorted foods, which they placed with aplomb in front of their guests. The guests were visibly impressed. Their hosts had prepared a variety of dishes: *achu*, *koki*, jolof rice, rice and beans, fufucorn, meat stew; I am telling you, food was abundant that year. The tables set, the birds prepared to quench their thirst and to appease their hunger when Tortoise loudly cleared his throat. The rustle of feathers quieted down. Tortoise cleared his throat once again.

"Before we eat, may I ask whom this food is for?" Tortoise inquired.

"For all of you," the hosts replied in unison.

Tortoise looked solemnly around him, made himself even more comfortable, and began to eat. He ate without haste. The more deliberately he ate, the angrier the birds became. Tortoise helped himself from one dish and the next while the others sat and watched. Their hosts could not understand such deference. Why was Tortoise eating alone? But he looked so different, with plumage they had never seen in the sky. The hosts concluded he must be their king; a leader who had the honor of eating while his subjects waited respectfully for him to finish his meal. Different people have different customs, they concluded, and watched Tortoise eat. At last, Tortoise asked for water to wash his hands, let out a loud belch, reclined in his chair, and began to pick his teeth with the tip of his tongue. There was barely anything left. The birds grudgingly fought over his pickings. Tortoise snored away contentedly. And so, at the conclusion of what was supposed to have been an end-of-year festival of gluttony and indulgence, the birds thanked their hosts and left for their long journey back to earth. As soon as they were out of earshot, a bitter quarrel broke out.

"I was suspicious when he asked us to change our names," Nshee flared up.

"You're right, Weaverbird. I don't know why we ever let that crook come with us. He completely ruined the festival this year," Mashii'mbaa-the-Palmbird complained bitterly.

Membenke-the-Crow did not listen to the litany of complaints. As far as she was concerned, this yearly feast was their private Xanadu, and Tortoise had irreversibly tarnished their enthusiasm. She deftly pulled her feather from Tortoise's shell and flew away. One by one, the other birds followed suit. Tortoise had anticipated trouble, but the idea of losing his feathers had not crossed his mind. Soon his shell was bare of its feathers. He looked at his naked shell and was quite at a loss. What will I do? he silently lamented. But Tortoise was never one to tally his losses. He had an idea. He asked his friend, Hawk, to carry a message to his wife. "Please tell her to put all the soft things we own outside on the *nsaa*," Tortoise implored. Hawk declined to take the message and flew off for earth. Tortoise spoke to the other birds. They all said no. Finally, Parrot offered to deliver the message. When he arrived at Tortoise's home, he told Mrs. Tortoise that her husband had requested she put all the hard objects they owned out in the yard. Mrs. Tortoise looked at Parrot and asked, "How is my husband?" Parrot looked at Mrs. Tortoise and said, "Oh, he is well. He ate a bit too much and couldn't keep up with us. He will be home soon enough." Mrs. Tortoise thanked Parrot and offered him some palm nuts. Parrot thanked her and flew away. Left alone, Mrs. Tortoise dutifully filled the *nsaa* with her mortar, pestle, grinding stone, cutlass, pots, pans, hoes—in short, everything they owned that was anything but soft.

Up in the sky, Tortoise waited and waited and waited, and then he jumped, falling to the earth. He fell and fell and fell. People say that for the first time in his life, Tortoise was stunned when he hit the *nsaa*. His shell shattered and the pieces scattered all over the compound. Tortoise was in agony; his entire body was lacerated and in excruciating pain. Mrs. Tortoise searched the entire compound and, one by one, she recovered all the pieces of her husband's shell. She carried her husband to the healer, Noghnegheb-the-Chameleon. Chameleon employed all his skills, and yet it took six moon cycles for Tortoise's wounds to heal. Chameleon glued his shell back together and sent him home. It is from that incident that Tortoise lost the smoothness of his shell. The birds say that as punishment, Tortoise will never regain it. For once he never saw it coming!

The story is finished.

The Story of Cat and Dog

Our people say that a man once killed his friend because of money; that because of a woman two brothers disowned one another; and that the friendship between Bushi-the-Cat and Mbo-the-Dog ended because of a gourd of honey.

It all happened when Cat and Dog, who had been friends from the beginning of time, went to the forest foraging for food. While they scoured the forest, they accidentally came upon a calabash of honey someone had hidden under some shrubs. The shrub cluster was in bloom, and the two friends were drawn to the bright red flowers. Dog quickly picked up the scent of honey and they were elated at their discovery. Dog suggested they hide their find and Cat agreed. Cat carried the calabash, scaled the trunk of a mahogany tree, and hid the honey well in a cluster of branches.

One day, Cat told his friend that his sister, the one who lived two villages away, had had a baby. He had to go and see the newborn. Dog congratulated his friend and said, "Tell your sister I broke my leg. That's why I didn't come with you. Tell her I'll come and see the baby when my leg has healed." Cat said good-bye to his friend and family and left one bright early morning. He made straight for the forest and ate half the honey they had hidden up in the tree. He sang on his way back home like an intoxicated man who had drunk too much palm wine at a death celebration.

"Welcome back, my friend. Did your in-law slaughter a cow?" Dog joked.

"No, but he killed a big cock for me," Cat declared, thumping his chest.

"Your sister and the newborn must be in good health."

"Indeed they are," Cat replied, standing ten inches taller.

"What's the name of the child?"

"Manoji."

"Ooh! It's a boy."

"Yes. What's a man without a male heir? Don't they say a stranger cannot be allowed to carry the corpse of a kinsman? My in-law will sleep peacefully now."

"You said it!"

Eight market weeks passed, and one Ntobah,[1] Cat informed his friend that his mother had just given birth and he wished to go and see the child. Once again Dog came up with an excuse. Cat's mother lived three villages away and Dog had no intention of trekking that far, so he said to Cat, "Tell your mother that I have a fever. That's the only reason why I didn't come with you to see the newborn." Early the next morning, Cat left for the forest, where he emptied the calabash. Sitting at home, Dog could hear his friend singing, his voice echoing across the hills beyond as he returned. Cat looked even happier this time and Dog knew he must have had a brother.

Moons passed and Christmas was drawing near. Dog reminded his friend that it was time to begin preparations for the feast. "We need to go get the honey from the forest," Dog suggested. Cat made no objections. The two friends walked hand-in-hand to the forest. Cat climbed up the tree, brought the calabash down and behold, it was empty.

[1]The Beba have an eight-day calendar cycle. The first day of that cycle, *Nkpezah,* is followed by *Ntobah, Ndzembebeh, Ndokuh, Nshialah, Webloh, Bamidzetoh,* and finally *Bamikoh.*

"What happened?" Cat looked pensive. "Do you think the honey could have evaporated?"

Hi hi hi hi hi—Dog laughed the laugh of a man who had just received news of the death of his firstborn son. "Who has ever heard of honey drying up? Besides, it hasn't been that hot this year," Dog hissed, the hyena in him taking over his emotions. "You, you must have eaten all the honey," Dog accused.

"When did I do such a hideous thing? I have not been near this forest since we last came here. Please be careful when you make such accusations . . ."

"You . . . I will say . . . you, you are a thief," Dog stammered. "You must have eaten the honey when you told me those stories about going to visit an imaginary nephew and brother. In fact, your sister's son-in-law, Antelope, husband to your eldest niece, told me his mother-in-law hasn't had a child in two years. As for your mother, that old hag, she is long past childbearing age . . . She can have children when I can fly!"

"You are lying, Dog. You know I haven't touched this honey."

"Of course you're the thief. They say it's because of rain that goats, hens, and chickens hide under the same roof. Well, you and I lived through a flood and right now, I never want to see you near my house again."

They quarreled over the honey and quarreled and quarreled because that was the only thing they could do. Dog was so angry and disappointed with Cat that their friendship indeed ended after this brawl over honey, something people remember to this day. Dog attacked Cat and broke Cat's jawbone. To this day, you can hear Cat meowing whenever it's cold because the wound never completely healed. The animals that helped stop the fight tried to reconcile them, but their efforts were wasted on those two. It is said that since that palaver over the honey Cat's and Dog's attitudes epitomize what the Beba mean by being bitter-in-the-throat. That calabash of honey became their ulcer, the type that continues to eat at your flesh long after you are dead. Cat and Dog never got over it, and they passed this ulcer down to generations of their children. That's why they're still sniping at each other to this day, and the Beba say nothing will ever change that.

The story is finished.

The Story of Monkey and Bee

Have you ever heard the saying that Antelope hates the person who reveals, even unintentionally, her hiding place more than the person who eventually traps or kills her? One of the animals in our story would agree with Antelope. That's none other than Nkierr-the-Monkey, who was friends with Nyo-the-Bee. It was one of those friendships that developed over something rather trivial. Bee was having a quiet nap. Monkey's children were swinging leisurely from branch to branch. They inadvertently woke up the sleeping Bee. Bee, still groggy from sleep, stung whoever had roused him from his afternoon slumber. Little Monkey's face ballooned and Bee felt sorry about what had happened. He stayed up at night watching over the whimpering child with Monkey. The three nights they nursed Little Monkey cemented the beginning of a long friendship. That's why they were often seen together.

They were of course together on this day when they went to visit Takro-the-Lion. Lion welcomed them warmly and offered them some food. Bee tasted the food and it went to his head. It was the best *egusi*[1] soup he had ever eaten: the ground pumpkin seeds had been blended with the right amount of *njama njama*[2]

[1]Pumpkin seeds in Pidgin English.

[2]A generic Pidgin English term for vegetables, it also applies to a type of vegetable popular in the grasslands, also known as huckleberry, and known among the Beba as *njankah.*

and peppers, the yellow ones he had always favored over the red ones. So smooth was the pounded cassava he could not detect a lump. Ancestors forbid! This food was so delicious that Bee decided he wanted it all for himself. He politely asked his friend Monkey to wash her hands before eating from the same bowl with him. Monkey was taken aback. Why such a request? This had never happened in all the years she had known Bee. Because she was quite hungry herself and didn't want to be disrespectful of their host, she poured some water in a dish and washed her hands. In fact, Monkey washed her hands thrice but they remained as black as ever. Bee would not relent. "Only death likes to eat with dirty hands," Bee grumbled and went right on eating. The more Monkey tried to clean her hands, the more she became frustrated by her best friend's ridicule. Sulking and bitter, Monkey departed, leaving Bee to enjoy the meal alone. She felt like the man in the story who was able to cross a big river only to later drown in a spring.

Our people are right when they say that life dances to the beat of the seasons. In the midst of one season we forget about the other until it is upon us. And so, time passed and our two friends went about their lives. To break the monotony, Monkey suggested they pay Ndafo-the-Tiger a visit. Tiger had not seen them since the last *nwa ngeh*, the annual communal cleansing ritual. He was therefore happy to see them. They arrived in the evening just as he finished making some *achu.*[3] Tiger did what our ancestors have done for millennia, what we continue to do to this day, and what our children will hand down to their children: he offered them some of his food and palm wine.

They had barely started eating when Monkey exclaimed, "Bee, my friend, you are making a lot of noise. How can we enjoy our meal with so much noise?" Monkey complained before Bee could taste the food. "I can't eat through this ruckus. If you don't stop making that noise, you won't touch a drop of

[3]Beba staple food made of pounded taro root.

this delicious *achu* soup." So saying, she swallowed a lump of *achu*, removed a piece of dry-meat, and stuffed her mouth. Bee couldn't stand watching her chew away so blithely.

Bee flew in and out of the house making every effort to be quiet but the more he buzzed around, the more noise he made. How can a bee be quiet when buzzing is the most apian of things, the sound of the drum he lives to beat? Bee screamed at Monkey. He felt like the owner of a he-goat who had just been impaled by the goat's horn. Monkey ate on, not saying a word. Bee felt defeated. He apologized to his friend, promising never again to mock another's nature. Monkey finished her meal. She then told Bee he was forgiven. And it is said that from that day Bee has kept a watchful eye, punishing with stinging swiftness those who make the same mistake he had made with his friend. Their families lived happily together from then on.

The story is finished.

The Foolish Leopard

A long time ago, a group of farmers lived in a land far, far away. These farmers grew different types of crops: plantains, cocoyams, bananas, yams, cassava, maize, pumpkins, *njankah*—sweet and bitter vegetables; in fact, anything that could grow in their earth, they planted. At home, they raised sheep, goats, pigs, and fowl. The young children who didn't go to the farms stayed at home during the day and tended to these animals. They were indeed a prosperous people, their harvest always plentiful. They could never consume all the food they had saved from the previous season before another harvest season would be upon them. There was just one problem these villagers had to contend with: although their harvest was plentiful, their animals rarely reached maturity. Countless *ngwaba'* lived in the neighboring woods. They came out at night and roamed through the village, killing and eating some of their animals. The farmers might have been good at tilling the soil; they might know when to look up into the sky, read the moisture in the clouds, and plant their seeds; they might know when to weed their crops in time for the flowering; but they were sadly a people who did not hunt. The earth was their sun. It shined during the day and breathed life into their plants. The earth was their moon. It shined bright at night and they told their children *ble* under large cotton trees. But they learned to leave the forest to its own devices at night. And the *ngwaba'* had learned to stalk the night and pay the village unwanted visits.

The farmers convened a meeting and decided to send some emissaries to a neighboring village, a village boasting men who were as good at hunting as they were at farming. As the Beba are wont to say, the emissaries gathered their things, and left as dusk fell. They reported their predicament to the hunters, who after listening to the calamity that had befallen their neighbors agreed to track down the leopards. They would take home all the leopards they killed as payment for their assistance. The hunters spent many wakeful nights, employed all their hunting skills, but failed to kill any leopards. These leopards behaved like human beings with a sixth sense. They would stand in the line of fire, staring straight at the hunters, but when the hunters fired their double-barrels the leopards seemed to know exactly when to disappear from sight. It seemed they were trying to prove to the hunters that only the owner of a mad dog knows how to catch it. Tired of losing precious gunpowder, the hunters decided to change tactics. They would lay traps instead. They selected eight spots around the village where they dug deep pits. They carefully covered the pits with dry twigs and grass. Nights came and went and the leopards went about the forest foraging for food as was their habit. They wondered why the humans had suddenly decided to leave the forest to them. As night turned into day and days faded into nights the leopards grew more and more suspicious of the humans. They convened a meeting and agreed not to venture into the village until they could sniff out what the humans were up to.

One day as it so happened, a very hungry *ngwaba'* ventured out during the daytime to look for food. As he wandered about the bushes near some cornfields, he caught sight of a *mbiandeb.* This rat mole was fat, hairy, and ran with a clumsy gait. Leopard shot after it but the rat mole quickly disappeared down a hole. In hot pursuit of the rat mole, Leopard failed to see one of the pit traps and fell straight into it. He tried unsuccessfully to plant his claws into the wall. His back hit the bottom of the pit, puum! And there Leopard languished. For two long days and two long nights the hunters did not come to inspect their traps. On the third day, to his delight, Leopard saw Nkierr swinging happily from branch to branch in the tree just above his head. He was beside himself. He called out to Monkey.

"My dear friend," he said in a wheedling voice, "help me. Please look down. I am trapped in this godforsaken human pit. Please come down and help me get out of this hole before those men come back to inspect their traps. I've been here for two days and I am starving."

"I know you, Leopard. If I help you, you will eat me," Monkey replied.

"Come, my friend. Why would I eat you? I won't dare do such a thing, not after you've saved my life. You know that rivers only fill up with water from the rain gutter. Please, please help me. Don't leave me here to die."

Monkey harvested a few leaves, chewed on them, and weighed Leopard's request. "I don't trust him," he thought. "You can never trust a leopard; not a hungry one in any case." He plucked yet another leaf and chewed on it. Leopard's eyes were red and weak; his breathing labored. Monkey knew it was only a matter of time and Leopard would meet his ancestors. He felt sorry for Leopard despite his reservations. He somehow believed in Leopard's sincerity. Monkey swung from branch to branch down the tree to the edge of the pit. He dangled his long tail into the hole. Leopard caught hold of it, planted his hind legs into the wall of the pit and slowly maneuvered himself out. But no sooner did he breathe fresh air than he clamped his teeth shut on Monkey's tail.

"I will eat you."

A shocked Monkey looked at Leopard and said, "Didn't you promise not to eat me?"

"You know a hungry man can't listen to reason. I have to eat you."

"But you gave me your word."

"I did swear not to eat you, but you know that I am very hungry, so I must eat you," Leopard replied.

"But you know the law."

"What law?" Leopard asked, still holding Monkey's tail firmly between his teeth.

"You know the law of the land that states you must pray before you eat a monkey or else maggots will eat your intestines."[1]

Leopard thought about the law for a brief moment. His stomach growled, his bowels rumbled. He couldn't remember this law. He even doubted there was any such law. Determined not to give up a free meal, he let go of Monkey's tail, closed his eyes and began to pray. As a Beba would say, Monkey asked his legs whether he had ever eaten a meal without sharing with them and they responded, "Never." With one powerful push his legs propelled him up up and up and Monkey flew to the top of the tree. When Leopard finished his prayer and opened his eyes, he was all alone. He looked up and saw Monkey sitting gingerly on a branch, wagging his busy tail at him. Leopard was so upset with his own foolishness that he jumped and stomped on the ground like a spoiled brat. "I shouldn't have trusted you," he moaned, digging his paws into the ground. Monkey laughed at him and he stomped even harder. In his fury, his hind legs hit a stick lying across the mouth of the pit. He lost his balance and *puum* he was back inside the pit. High up in the tree, Monkey observed Leopard's antics, laughing and slapping his sides.

"You were right, my friend. It is the fly that makes feces popular," Monkey rebuked him and swung higher up into the tree.

[1]"Maggots will eat your intestines" is a Beba expression meaning, "You will have chronic diarrhea."

Monkey's laughter drew the attention of Akwoghnjob, who was grazing on that side of the hill. Cow chewed on some fresh grass and trotted over to the place of commotion.

"What's the matter with you today, little one?" she asked, looking up at Monkey.

"Hi hi hi, what can I say?" Monkey replied, still laughing and wiping the tears from his eyes.

"Something must have happened to make you this ebullient."

"You will not believe me if I tell you the truth."

"Look, my little *nkierr*, do I look like someone born yesterday? Does the gray of my hoof look like the color of those clouds?"

"All right, I'll tell you what happened . . . on one condition."

"What's that?"

"You must promise not to laugh."

"Out with it, you little rascal."

And so, Monkey told Cow the story about his encounter with the ungrateful Leopard; how Leopard wanted to eat him after he had saved his life. To Monkey's surprise, Cow mooed and mooed and mooed until the other animals heard the sound of her hooves stomping the earth.

"But you promised you weren't going to laugh."

"Yes, I did make that promise. You don't actually think that I believe you, do you?"

"What do you mean?"

"I mean . . . you want me to believe that a puny thing like you helped Leopard out of this pit?"

"I swear I did exactly as I am telling you."

Cow mooed to the edge of the pit, stared straight at Leopard, looked up at Monkey, and said, "Is this the one you say you helped?"

Monkey swung to the ground, walked over to the pit, peered inside, and nodded vigorously at Cow.

"You really take me for a fool, don't you? You expect me to believe that someone as tiny as you helped someone as large as this out of that hole? If it's really true that you did it, I want to see you do it again," Cow sneered. Leopard seemed to have forgotten his hunger while watching the two talking over his head. A bemused smile danced on his lips. Monkey hesitated, but it was the kind of hesitation that one abandons because there was too much pride in his little stomach. Strength wasn't always about size. This he was bent on proving to Cow. Monkey planted his buttocks on the ground and lowered his tail into the pit. Leopard caught hold of it, quickly dug his claws into the wall, and crawled out of the pit. No sooner was he out than he stuck his teeth into Monkey's butt.

"Leopard, what are you doing?" Monkey cried.

"I am hungry. I haven't eaten in two days and now I must eat you . . ."

But before he could bite into Monkey flesh, Cow burst out laughing. She mooed even louder than she had before. Leopard and Monkey were both surprised at her behavior.

"Is something wrong?" Leopard asked, grabbing Monkey's butt with his right paw.

"I can't believe what I am seeing," Cow said. "Is it really possible that a little thing like Monkey can pull you out of a hole?"

"You saw it with your own eyes," Leopard retorted.

"No. I need to see this one more time so that when I tell the others I'll know my eyes didn't fool me the first time."

"What? You want me to get back into the pit?"

"Yes."

"Look, I haven't eaten in two days and I need to eat this monkey."

"You better hurry then. The sooner you're in, the sooner you're back out, the sooner you can eat and the sooner I'll be on my way."

"Fine," Leopard said and jumped into the pit.

To his surprise, Cow fell on her butt, raised her front legs in the air and laughed and laughed and laughed. Monkey was nowhere to be found. From high up in the tree he pointed at Leopard and declared, "One good turn deserves another. Where have you ever heard of a child who slaps the mother or bites the breast that feeds it? You shall end up in a pot today, you fool." And Monkey laughed, swinging away from branch to branch, leaving Leopard to his fate.

This story is finished.

Tiger Kills His Mother

Ndafo-the-Tiger and Torokee-the-Tortoise were once very good friends. Their friendship had survived the year of the locusts, and it seemed it would survive the famine that was currently ravaging their land. It had happened unexpectedly. The rains had suddenly ceased. One would think adequate sacrifices had not been offered to the gods. There was even talk that some elders had forsaken the libations due their ancestors. It was thus a time of starvation and the animals roamed the forest foraging for the little food they could find. Sometimes it took days to find something to eat. Some simply collapsed and died. As the drought dragged on, the animals grew leaner and leaner. Their bones began to show through their skin. It was clear that if the rains did not return sometime soon, the animals would turn on each other. And so, Tortoise went to bed each night and toyed with an idea. He was going to propose to Tiger that they kill and eat their mothers. He had expected Tiger's support but was surprised when his friend vehemently protested.

"But they're both very old. They don't have much time left anyway," Tortoise argued.

"No, that's an abomination. Not even a prolonged drought warrants the death of our mothers. I will spill my mother's blood over my dead body."

"They are old. Would you rather we died? They have lived long, fruitful lives. Why should we leave this world before them?"

"You have a point," Tiger ventured. Tiger loved his mother, but when he looked at his emaciated body the hunger devoured his desire to protect her.

"I have a plan," Tortoise explained. "We will go to the river. I will take my mother upstream and you will take yours downstream. I will kill my mother. When you see the water red with her blood, only then should you kill your mother. Remember, you must wait until the river is red with my mother's blood."

The friends took the path leading to the river. They arrived at the pool at that time of day when the animals used to sunbathe when life was bountiful. Here they parted ways. Tortoise walked upstream and Tiger walked downstream. Tortoise harvested some *baanjob*, ground the leaves on a stone and squeezed its red juices into a bowl; you know, the type of juices from *baanjob* that women use to dye cloth and whose flowers teenage girls use to paint their lips and color their palms. He carried the bowl and emptied its contents into the river. When Tiger saw the water, red with Mother Tortoise's blood, he picked up his cutlass and with one blow chopped off his mother's head. The deed done, Ndafo whistled and Torokee joined him. Thanks to all the fallen trees and broken branches littering the forest, the two friends easily gathered a bundle of firewood. Tortoise offered Tiger the bag of cocoyams he had brought along for their meal. Tiger gladly peeled and cooked a delicious pot of cocoyam porridge.

"This meat is a bit tough," Tortoise commented through mouthfuls. The two friends were eating in silence, watching the river flowing down into the valley.

"I told you they were old enough," Tortoise again broke the silence. Tiger simply nodded and kept on eating.

The next day, it was Tortoise's turn to provide a meal. Tiger gave him some plantain, which Tortoise used to cook *sese*. Tiger sat down with his friend and enjoyed a sumptuous plantain porridge meal. "Your mother tastes quite soft, the old hag," Tiger commented through mouthfuls. "Yes, but I spent a lot more time cooking her than you did your mother." What Tiger did not know was that Tortoise had caught some squirrels the day before. He had kept them hidden in the bush before making the deal with Tiger. He had also hid his mother in the abandoned *ntso*[1] palm bush close to the river. Tiger ate quietly, watching the river flow peacefully on its own journey. But chronic hunger has a way of taunting one that a good meal in a time of famine is just that, one inconsiderate appeaser. The smells of a meal followed you as you walked the dry paths in search of the berries you wouldn't touch when times are good; the sight of dry twigs would make your mouth water for they remind you of the old brittle bones you had chewed and swallowed without haste. It didn't take long for Tiger to notice something strange about his friend. Tortoise adopted the queer attitude of excusing himself and taking off alone after their meager meals. "I'll be right back," he'd say and always insisted on going alone. Tiger was puzzled nonetheless by his friend's behavior. One day, Tiger secretly followed Tortoise to the *ntso* bush and saw him giving food to his mother. "So that's what you've been up to, my friend," Tiger whispered, elated his suspicions had been right. He knew his friend was full of cunning but how was he to suspect that Tortoise could dupe him in a matter concerning the mothers who had given them life? He ran, making sure he got home before Tortoise returned. A week passed. One bright sunny Ntobah, Tortoise asked his friend to accompany him on a food hunt.

[1]Raffia palms are common to the Bamenda region of the North West Province. *Ntso* are of the raffia palm family but they are different. They grow abundantly in the Beba semiforest region. They are lower to the ground than palm trees but are much bigger and taller than raffia palms. Raffia palms can be tapped at ground level but one almost always has to use a ladder in order to tap the *ntso*. Raffia, *ntso*, and palm trees produce palm wine, each with a distinctive taste.

"I am not feeling well today," Tiger lied.

"What is wrong with you?" a concerned Tortoise asked.

"I've had a pain in my back for the past three days."

"You'd better lie down," Tortoise replied. "At least it's not a fever. Rest, I'll see you when I get back."

"May your luck be bountiful today," Tiger invoked their ancestors.

No sooner had Tortoise left for the forest than Tiger took off for the palm bush where he found Tortoise's mother. He killed the old woman, cooked the meat with some cocoyams and ate the meal all alone, his eyes fixed on the river flowing to its destination of no-return. Tortoise came home quite exhausted and went directly to sleep. The next day after their morning meal, he excused himself and went on yet another I'll-be-right-back trip. Tiger could usually hear him whistling or singing when he returned from each trip. Today, Tortoise came home looking very sick.

"You're running a fever," a concerned Tiger said, placing one hand on his friend's brow. "Here, lie down. Get some rest. I'll go look for some fever-grass."

Tortoise remained bedridden for a fortnight. He wouldn't eat. When he did eat he threw everything up. Tiger was alarmed by the prospect of losing his friend. He multiplied the fever-grass treatments, forcing Tortoise to sweat away the fever. Tiger even prayed for Tortoise's recovery. Without warning, strong winds blew blankets of dust into the air and the rains began to fall again. At last Tortoise began to regain his appetite and his mood improved as life returned to the land. The two friends went on with their lives, the drought now a memory. The farming season was uneventful. The heavy rains came after the harvest and the land rested. In no time, the dry season was knocking on their doors and the animals rejoiced at the expectation of a good hunting season. One hazy, dull morning, Tortoise woke up, yawned and spoke to his friend.

"Have you prepared your hunting ground yet?"

"No, not yet."

"I think we should do that in the next two weeks," Tortoise proposed. "You stake out an area, I'll stake out mine and we'll help each other with the hunt."

"That's a good idea. We'll catch more game if we work together. Just make sure you find a good area," Tiger joked.

"I will," Tortoise promised.

The two friends staked out their hunting grounds. When they were both ready they took off one bright morning, each carrying a *nswa*[2] and a cutlass. They chatted and laughed, the laughter of babies who'd been home all day with young siblings and suddenly saw their weary mothers walk through the door. They hadn't been this happy in a long time.

"When we get there, one of us has to stand in the middle of the hunting parcel, light the fire, and the other will wait for the animals to escape the fire . . ."

"Isn't that dangerous?" Tiger queried. "Wouldn't the person who lights the fire get burnt to death?"

"Not at all," Tortoise responded confidently. "If you're that worried let's begin with my plot."

Ndafo was reassured by his friend's cocksure attitude. What was the point in arguing with him? What do I stand to lose if he dies in his fire? Tiger reflected. His mother had often told him that arrogant people always give their enemies the tools with which to destroy them, so he smiled instead and told his friend, "I am ready."

Tortoise sauntered to the middle of his hunting ground and lit the fire. The dry grass and twigs burned quickly. No sooner did the smoke circle above their heads than Tiger heard the animals running for their lives. He dashed about, running along the path Tortoise had made encircling his hunting ground. He furiously clubbed to death as many animals as he could. Tiger

[2]A net bag.

sat down, inspecting the catch. He was taken aback when his friend's voice broke into his thoughts.

"What a great catch we've got here," Tortoise said in an off-handed manner, pointing at the game lying at Tiger's feet. There were rat moles, many of those grass-cutters the Beba call *njome*, a few anteaters, and a deer. "This meat will last us at least a week."

"You're right," Tiger answered limply. He couldn't hide his surprise at seeing his friend. Tortoise smiled. He did not reveal to his friend that while they were preparing their hunting grounds he had secretly dug a tunnel from his plot to the edge of the forest. He had simply slipped down that hole as soon as he started the fire and waited for the commotion to end. The two friends put all the game into their *nswa* and after a long trek arrived home with their heavy loads. They lazily spent the week eating chunks of meat, swimming in the pool, and sleeping the days out on the rocks, basking in the sun. But a week of such abandon usually fades away rather quickly. The two friends had to go back to the hunt, this time on Tiger's parcel of land. Tiger walked to the middle of the plot and lit his fire. Hot flames leaped into the air and the fire burned fiercely. Tiger became hysterical once the grass started burning and the animals were escaping for their lives. Tortoise was busy clubbing away while the flames licked Tiger's face and singed his skin. Soon Tiger could smell the fat of his own flesh burning.

"This fire is too hot," he complained. "I have to get out of these flames," he screamed.

"No, you can't," Tortoise replied and started stoning his friend. "You must stay there until all the grass and twigs burn out just like I did."

"If I stay here any longer, I will die."

"If I stay here any longer I will die," Tortoise mimicked Tiger, imitating the cries of a baby. "Die! . . . Who told you that my mother deserved to die by your hand, you idiot . . . Die!"

Tortoise screamed and threw even bigger stones at Tiger. And so Ndafo died at Torokee's hand. Torokee went home happy that he had avenged his mother's death.

The story is finished.

A Tug-of-War

Torokee had a big mouth. All the animals in the kingdom knew that. He would boast about things he had done such as tricking and killing Ndafo and his mother the year of the famine. He would brag about the things he planned to do, including flying to the sky for the annual feast of the birds. No wonder the animals admired him, but some envied and even hated him. They resented the way he crawled around the forest like a snail in labor but always found a way to outwit them in a time of crisis. The animals thought they had heard it all from Tortoise until the day he openly challenged Nserr-the-Elephant to a duel.

"Have you heard?" Surprise spread from lip to lip. "Have you heard that Torokee has challenged mighty Nserr to a tug-of-war?" tongues wagged.

"Yes. They say he walked up to Elephant and told him that he was all fat and no bones. He even called Elephant the biggest coward in the kingdom."

"Tortoise has a big mouth, but I don't believe even he could have said that."

Indeed Tortoise had told Elephant, "You think you're so big and so strong! Only empty wind blows behind those ears. Let's have a tug-of-war. I'll prove to you that I am stronger than you are," he had said with characteristic superciliousness. Elephant looked at Tortoise and flapped his giant ears until the wind blew Tortoise off his feet. Tortoise picked himself up and repeated the challenge. Only then did Elephant laugh and laugh until tears rolled down his face; some said the tears flowed out of his big ears.

"One hundred of you cannot challenge me," Elephant rebuffed him.

"Size does not equal strength. And by the way, it's not true that a mountain and another mountain can never meet," Tortoise retorted.

"What? You, a mountain? Meet me in four days then . . . on Ndzembebeh . . . at *gbweshi.*" Elephant impatiently dismissed Tortoise.

"The market square it is," Tortoise murmured, waddling off to the watering hole.

The next day, Tortoise went to the river for a cool drink. He ambled down the bank to the spot where the fat river beast, the one known as Nye-Nki, was having a laid-back swim.

"Who are you to churn up the water when I am drinking?" Tortoise scolded.

Hippopotamus opened his jaws wide and bawled, "Look here, you twit! Who do you think you are talking to?"

"I am talking to you. You don't scare me. Never mind your size; size isn't strength."

Hippopotamus lazily squirted water bubbles through his nostrils, ignoring Tortoise.

"I came here to challenge you to a fight. I will show you how strong I am. In case you think you are really that powerful, you should meet me here in three days."

"Meet you here in three days? . . . I live here. Now get out of the water," Hippopotamus barked, his massive jaws sinking into the muddy waters.

On Ndzembebeh, Tortoise trotted with fanfare to the square, dragging a long piece of rope. An entourage of animals surrounded him to the front and to the back. Some blew on their horns, others whistled, and the rest hollered all the way to *gbweshi.* He found Elephant leaning against a tree trunk scratching the fleas feeding on his skin. He was so intent on what he was doing that no one dared disturb him. He flapped his ears, silencing the animals. They stopped a good distance away from Elephant. They waited, watching to see what Tortoise would do. Some were already feeling sorry for Tortoise. Others were unsympathetic. They'd had enough of Tortoise's high jinks. They simply smiled, hoping for a story they'd live to tell their descendants for generations to come.

Tortoise dragged the rope over to Elephant, handed him one end of the rope, and said, "I am going to walk over to the other end of *gbweshi.* Start pulling when you see the rope shaking," he instructed. Tortoise sauntered as only Tortoise could across the square to loud jeers from the crowd. He disappeared down the slope to the rock where Nye-Nki was resting by the river bank. He didn't bother to greet Hippopotamus.

"Take this. Start pulling when you see the rope shaking," he commanded, giving Hippopotamus the other end.

He then ran up the little slope and shook the bight of the rope. Elephant and Hippopotamus saw the ripple. "Pull!" the bystanders shouted. The two giants started pulling. They pulled and pulled and pulled. Soon they were out of breath and exhausted. Elephant fell against the tree trunk and Hippopotamus collapsed onto the rock. Tortoise ran down the slope to Hippopotamus.

"Why did you stop?"

"I am tired. I need some rest."

"Are you saying that I am stronger than you are?"

"I said I need some rest. Now go away," Hippopotamus growled, and his powerful jaws disappeared under the water. Tortoise walked up the slope to the gathering and confronted Elephant. The animals again surrounded Tortoise and in no time there was a crowd.

"Why did you stop?"

"I am tired. I need some rest."

"You? You need some rest because you couldn't pull a little rope with me? Haven't I heard it said that an elephant is never defeated by the weight of its tusks?" Tortoise mocked.

"Yes. And a maiden's breasts are never too heavy for her to carry. You have neither breasts nor tusks. Now go away," Elephant raised his trunk into the air and hollered.

The animals stampeded in all directions. Tortoise whistled all the way home and told his wife about his victory over the two giants.

"How can you be stronger than Nserr and Nye-Nki, my husband?"

"Knowledge is strength, my wife. Knowledge is strength," Tortoise chuckled.

The story is finished.

The Race

The Beba have a saying that one who has a sibling is never beaten to death. It is also said that in the animal kingdom, Tswe-the-Hare and Torokee-the-Tortoise were never friends. Some contend their dislike for each other was legendary. Apparently, this all seemed to be rooted in the innocent games children play. Torokee's children have for generations taunted Tswe's children, calling their tiny legs broomsticks fit for lighting forest fires, telling them humans would love to use their broomsticks to sweep the dry leaves around their *nsaa.* Tswe's children fight their tormentors but always lose because their foes have the cruel habit of pulling their heads and legs into their shells to deflect Tswe's children's kicks. Adding insult to injury, the young Tswe have to bear the sardonic Torokee laughter when they hurt themselves against hard shells. Knowing this, the animals murmured that Hare would one day teach Tortoise a bitter lesson, but the opportunity to finally settle this score took them all by surprise.

It was that time of the year when food was abundant and the animals, like the humans, had all taken in a good harvest. From sunrise to sunset, from sunset to sunrise, the animals roamed the fields and the forests and ate their fill. They grew fat; their females bore healthy litters, and they listened to the young ones fill the forest with their hungry cries and playfulness. They knew angry humans would come after them, but in a time of plenty many more survived than would have otherwise. Losing some of their family members was part of the cycle of life they had come to accept. The humans rested and celebrated with drums and dancing and eating: those who had postponed the death celebration of a loved one seized on this time of rest to display their wealth and honor their dead ancestors; men would dance the *ndo'to* and women, the *ndzang*. Young human females would organize *fembwerr* dances where young men courted them, professed their love, proposed to them, and later married them and had children. It was also their custom to perform the *nwa ngeh* festival to thank their gods and bless their homesteads.

With humans caught up in such serious matters, the animals indulged in their own festivities. Every year, they selected an event in which they could all partake. The previous year, they had celebrated with the animals of the neighboring village, and the year before that they had organized a hunting expedition in the forest for honey and termites because their females had been unusually blessed with young ones. Needless to say, the honey supposedly collected for the children was all eaten by the adults. There was a lot of excitement in the air this particular year because of the main event. It had all happened by accident. Their king, Takro the Lion, had called a meeting to discuss the upcoming festival. Torokee was uncharacteristically late for this meeting. And naturally, he wouldn't keep his mouth shut. His rude interruptions angered some of the animals, who immediately began rebuking him. "If you had not been born with lead in your legs you would've been here on time like everyone else," Tswe snorted. "If you think the gods blessed you with nimble legs then I challenge you to a race," Torokee shot back. The animals perked their ears. They batted eyelids at each other. Leopard coughed, Rabbit sneezed, and suddenly laughter broke out. The animals fell on their backs, threw their paws in the air, and laughed so hard a chorused vibration shook the forest. You would think someone had told them that humans had agreed at their *nwa ngeh* ceremony never to hunt animals again. Tswe was the first to recover. He asked Torokee to repeat what he had said. And there was Torokee shooting off his big mouth, repeating his challenge.

"Have you ever heard the expression, never compete with an elephant in defecating?" Tswe scowled.

"Or he probably hasn't heard the saying that he who befriends a fly or a beetle is brought presents of feces or dung."

"If it pleases those assembled here, these old and brittle legs are ready to run a race with Tswe," Torokee repeated his challenge. "You all seem to have forgotten the saying that clouds do not always forecast rain."

"This year a race between Torokee and Tswe will mark the end of our festivities. Go prepare yourselves!" Takro solemnly declared, drawing the meeting to a close.

"The crab does not realize there are two kinds of water until it is inside a pot," Leopard concluded. The animals dispersed.

Tswe left the meeting feeling a bit uneasy and insulted by Torokee's dare. But as the evening wore on he began to feel happy, even euphoric. What was he worried about? Why should he let something as trivial as a race with Torokee bother him? Wasn't he the fastest animal of the jungle? He slowly regained his confidence. Tswe laughed at what he clearly thought was blatant short-sightedness; foolishness, even, on Torokee's part. That one has fooled and tricked one too many animals in the past. It isn't going to happen this time, the animals gossiped. They tuned their drums, they rehearsed songs, and Tswe slept happily each of those long-drawn-out festive nights, not wasting a thought on the upcoming race.

Torokee spent his time visiting all the members of his family. He was so involved with them that some animals joked he must be saying his good-byes. Some openly wondered whether he'd survive all those trips. They say a single stick smokes but does not burn. Torokee plotted and planned for the race with his sons, daughters, aunts, uncles, grandparents; he talked to all who considered themselves his kinsfolk. When they were all satisfied with each one's contribution to the festivities, Torokee slept for an entire day.

Soon, the day of the race was upon them. Young drummers welcomed the animals from far and wide, and their companions sang the praises of the two contestants. They, along with Nserr, awaited Tswe's and Torokee's arrival at the starting line. Takro and the rest of the animals awaited the winner at the finish line. Tswe kicked his hind legs, waiting impatiently as Torokee clawed his way to the starting line amidst jeers and cheers. Finally, Nserr raised his trunk and his horn boomed across the forest. A loud cheer from the other end acknowledged the start of the race. Tswe shot off like a hunter's hungry arrow. He had one thought in mind, to teach a pompous Torokee a lesson. For once I'll be the one to do it; to finally save face for all the animals who have been humiliated generation after generation, he mumbled as he ran. He ran and ran and ran. When he got to the first stream he stopped for a drink. He drank three mouthfuls in quick succession. He then slowly lowered his head, stuck his tongue into the water and delicately lifted his head toward the sky. The more he repeated the movement, the more he admired his face in the water. He admired his left profile and then his right profile. He was so caught up admiring his reflexion that he almost fell into the stream. This made him laugh. He regained his balance and gingerly stuck his right leg into the river; then the left one. He was soon bored with the water, though feeling quite refreshed. He crossed the stream. He barely ran a few hundred yards when he heard the grass rustle. The noise startled him. He turned around to see who was intruding on his tranquillity. He was even more distressed when the intruder turned out to be Torokee. Tswe was stunned. Without saying a word, he took off again running as fast as he could until he reached the second stream. This time, he crossed over to the other side and then stopped for drink. Feeling very refreshed and confident that he had put a day's difference between Torokee and himself, he decided to take a nap. Tswe slept the hours away, occasionally yawning and scratching himself. He woke at that time of the day when the shadow is almost a foot long. It was time to be on his way. This time he didn't have to run. He simply ambled on, stopping and eating blades of grass to wade off the boredom. He was happily chewing soft green shoots when the sight of Torokee ahead almost blinded him. How did this happen? I must have overslept. Idiot! he admonished himself. "Not to worry, I'll make up for that sleep in no time," he shouted at Torokee, and took off once again. He finally arrived at nki Mbu, the big river close to the Tree of Victory. He relaxed, ignored the bridge, and *chuum!* somersaulted into the river. Sheets of clear water dug into his pelt and tickled his hide. He rolled over and over, keeping his head above water. A group of *mbwe* heard the commotion. Intrigued, they swam over to inspect this stranger in their pool. "Who are you?" the fishes asked. "I am Tswe," he replied. "And what are you doing here?" they asked. "I am running a race with Torokee." "You?" "Yes." "Why?" "He challenged me to a race, that's why." "But aren't you supposed to be the fastest animal in your land?" "Yes, I am." "Why would Torokee challenge you, then?" "He is pigheaded that way," Tswe replied. "And you were pigheaded enough to accept?" The fishes swam closer. They began admiring the brown and white shades of Tswe's skin. He was so taken with their admiration that he spent hours with the fishes telling them stories about the animals that lived on land. The *mbwe* in turn shared stories of water creatures. He was floating on his back, listening to the fishes when suddenly, they disappeared. It happened so swiftly Tswe wondered why they had vanished. What had he done to scare them away? He didn't have to wait long for an answer. He flipped over on his stomach, only to see Hippopotamus gliding silently into the pool. Tswe had not felt the vibration or seen the bubbles. Tswe leaped out of the pool onto the riverbank. He stared down at Nye-Nki.

"Why aren't you at the finish line?" Tswe shouted down at him.

"Don't pretend to be brave with me," Nye-Nki scoffed. "What are you doing here when Torokee is well on his way to winning your stupid race?"

"That is impossible. I left him two streams away when my shadow was still a foot long."

Nye-Nki gave Tswe a bored look, and his huge fangs disappeared from sight. Tswe was determined to win and so he banished any thoughts of Nye-Nki's condescending look. The more he ran, the more he sweated, the more he tired himself out. The more he ran, the more Torokee's rump came into full view. Torokee's sudden surge of speed was a mystery to Tswe, but he did not have the luxury to worry about that. He would never know that Torokee had strategically positioned family members along the race track. For whenever Tswe tired and turned around to see what distance separated him from his competition, he saw Torokee right behind him or in front of him. He redoubled his efforts. He could now hear the animals talking loudly and chanting their names. He was a few hundred yards from the Tree of Victory when deafening applause rose from the crowd of onlookers gathered underneath. Tswe slowed his pace, raised his head, cracked a huge smile and sauntered toward the thunder. A familiar noise chilled his stride. Grass rustled in a nearby copse and they all turned to see an exhausted-looking Torokee stagger to victory. Tswe arrived too late. Torokee had indeed beaten him. Takro declared Torokee the winner. Nserr lowered his trunk, scooped Torokee up, and lifted him high into the air above the crowd. The animals roared their applause. Some were astounded by this turn of events. In the commotion, it seems they had all forgotten the saying that Mother Red-Crab and her children all look alike.

The story of the race is finished.

Part 2

Metse-Tsate-Nfo, aka Sense-Pass-King

A long time ago, Nfo[1] Atabe ruled over a large kingdom. He was an arrogant and authoritative man. A man who wanted every festival, every monument, every funeral, every marriage or birth celebration, every ceremonial activity performed in his kingdom to bear his name or the mark of his authority. Ancestors forfend! He went as far as dispossessing families of one of their most sacred duties: the naming of their children. Tegheh kwu! Atabe decreed he would name all the children born under his reign. Men gnashed their teeth and cursed the king between gulps of palm wine. Naming children was the most sacred of male traditions; so it had been with their fathers, their grandfathers, and their forefathers. Men were born to uphold the father's lineage, a duty they carefully sustained by bestowing family names on their children. It was a sad time for these men. Like dogs, they tucked their tails between their legs, gnashed their teeth, and held their heads in shame.

It so happened that a woman had a baby boy and in accordance with Nfo Atabe's edict, she strapped her child on her back and made for the palace. She had not descended two hills and crossed two streams when she heard her son speak.

"Mother, let's go home," he said. "Why should the fon name me? Don't I have fathers, mothers, uncles, grandparents? Tegheh kwu! Dead-Father-of-Mine! The fon will not name me. My name is Metse-Tsate-Nfo."

[1]Among the Beba: the fon or king; a traditional ruler.

The woman was dumbfounded. "How is this possible? How is it that my child can speak?" she kept asking herself. "My son is merely a baby," she mumbled. "Why does he say his name is Metse-Tsate-Nfo? Why does he claim to be more intelligent than the king? This is unheard of. A child smarter than the king?" She gathered her anxiety, as the Beba say, in her palms, turned around, and walked back home. But she feared for her son. She feared the king's wrath. She had to, for it is said that the prince who is always looking at the throne is the first to be banished from the palace. She kept the truth about her son from the king.

Years passed and the news finally got to the Nfo Atabe that a woman named Manele did have a child. A son. The king learned that Manele's child, oh abomination, had named himself. What's more, he called himself Metse-Tsate-Nfo, meaning Intelligence-Greater-Than-the-King's, or Sense-Pass-King, as he was affectionately called in Pidgin English. Sense-Pass-King. How brazen! How fearless! How impertinent! Nfo Atabe would have none of it. He was so enraged by the news that he decided to teach this unrepentant, pretentious sapling a lesson. This so-called Metse-Tsate-Nfo had to learn that he wasn't above the law of the land—*his* law. The punishment for this upstart was death, he declared. He had to make an example of him.

One day, Nfo Atabe summoned Metse-Tsate-Nfo to the palace. The *ntsendia*[2] notified the boy that the fon's order was to bring him to the palace. "Why?" the boy asked. "The sovereign wants you to give him a haircut," the *ntsendia* confided. Metse-Tsate-Nfo was taken aback by this request. Nfo had special barbers, why send for him? Why bestow such an honor on a mere commoner? A mere boy for that matter. The *ntsendia* had no answers for the young man.

"I am only a message bearer," the *ntsendia* replied. "When the king asks me to take a message to one of his subjects, I do not question his motives."

[2]Nfo's messenger(s) or retainer(s).

Metse-Tsate-Nfo boiled some fresh corn and put a couple of ears in his bag, and the two men left for the palace. He arrived at the palace and was cordially welcomed by the king. King Atabe laid out an array of razors in front of the young man. Metse-Tsate-Nfo took his place by the king's side. Before he began his duty, Metse-Tsate-Nfo coughed into cupped hands, stepped in front of the king, and removed two warm maize cobs from his bag. He offered them to the king. The sweet aroma, the smell of baby-palm wine that young women typically like to drink, soon filled the room. Nfo Atabe accepted the gift. He didn't call for his tasters before sinking his teeth into the corn. Nfo Atabe quietly savored the succulent ears of sweet corn while Metse-Tsate-Nfo cut his hair. When the young barber announced he had finished his job, King Atabe smiled the smile of a wearisome hunter who at the end of a long night in the forest finds a helpless deer in his last trap.

"My son, have you finished?"

"Yes, *Mbeh*."[3]

"Is it well done?"

"I think Your Majesty will like it."

Atabe laughed that throaty patrician laugh of a demigod before addressing Sense-Pass-King. "Now my son, I want you to put all my hair back on my head."

"*Mbeh*, did I hear you correctly?"

"I said I order you to put my hair back on my head."

"Why, Your Majesty?"

Nfo Atabe chuckled again and said, "First, you've done something you should never have done: shorn the king's head of his hair. You are not a *nkwob;*[4] you are not a kingmaker. How dare you presume to be so bold? Second, if you do not do what I ask of you right now, you shall die at sunset."

[3]Respectful form of address; only the fon or chief or king can be addressed as such; the nfo is never directly called by name to his face, hence, *Mbeh.*

[4]A noble; plural, *bekwob.*

"*Mmmmmbeh,*" Metse-Tsate-Nfo stammered. "Can a child re-enter its mother's womb after it has been born?"

"I do not argue with children," Atabe snapped. "I want my hair back on my scalp or you lose yours at sundown."

"Great King, if that is your wish, I will do it on one condition . . ."

"You are lucky I am in a good mood today . . . Speak!"

"I will do it on one condition, my lord. I want you to put all the grains of corn you ate while I was shaving your hair back on the cob. Once that's done, your hair will be safely back on your head."

The *nstendia* and *bekwob* who had been watching the drama unfold hid their mouths in their palms and laughed heartily at the young man. Atabe would not publicly chastise his bodyguards and nobles, so he laughed even louder. When his laughter settled he asked one of his *ntsendia* to bring him five young piglets. The fon selected four young men and gave each of them a piglet. He gave the last one to Metse-Tsate-Nfo.

"Take your gift home with you and raise it. At the end of each year you must each bring me a pig," the fon ordered.

The boys were so happy to have been singled out by the king that each year they dutifully took a pig to the palace; all of them except of course Sense-Pass-King. The first year came and went and the second and the third. Atabe was fed up with this young man and summoned him again to the palace. This time people were convinced Sense-Pass-King would be banished from the kingdom. They all assembled at the palace but the accused was nowhere in sight. They waited all day. He still didn't show up. Dusk was approaching and people were beginning to gather their things to begin their journeys home when Metse-Tsate-Nfo ran huffing and puffing into the courtyard.

"You have openly defied your king. The penalty is death," Atabe declared.

"But my lord, I am late because I was assisting my father, who was having a baby."

"What? How can a man have a baby? You have insulted this palace one too many times."

"But Mbeh, a man can have a baby the same way the male pig you gave me can."

The people cheered and an angry Nfo Atabe dismissed the crowd. Moons passed and the villagers forgot about the boy who had outsmarted their leader. But a nasty rumor began to spread throughout the land. Nfo Atabe had ordered that a stage be built right there in front of the palace. The story went that the king was planning on mounting a big chair on this throne; he would grant Metse-Tsate-Nfo the honor of being crowned the most intelligent person in the kingdom. "Sense-Pass-King is going to be honored; Sense-Pass-King is going to be honored by the king," the gossip passed from lip to lip and drum to drum. Once again, Metse-Tsate-Nfo wondered why he deserved this honor. His curiosity grew as preparations gained momentum. Eager to know more, he started digging a secret passage from his house to the palace. He was not surprised when he discovered that the coronation chair would sit on top of a pit.

The sun was bright, the air brisk, the people festive on Metse-Tsate-Nfo's big day. The young man wore the best embroidered *tob*[5] the villagers had ever seen and whistled his way to the palace. Indeed, he looked like a prince, an heir to the throne in that black and red *tob*. The coronation chair was equally finely covered with the expensive black cotton cloth known as *ndip*. Back then, as today, *ndip* was used only for special occasions. A bachelor who gives *ndip* to his future in-laws, no matter the occasion, makes an important statement about his status or ability to take care of his future family. Nfo Atabe had spared no expense. He meant this to be a grand event indeed. First he made a lengthy speech, praising Metse-Tsate-Nfo.

[5]Free-flowing gown or boubou worn by men; sometimes made with rich intricate embroidered designs; often worn for ceremonial purposes or on important occasions.

"When a child's parents or guardians are still alive it dances and snaps its toes. When drummers change the beat of the drum, so will dancers change their dance step. They say a lazy man remembers he has not planted any crops only when his neighbors begin their harvest. We know the young man I am honoring today is the exact opposite of such a lazy man. That's why we're all here to pay tribute to this beacon of tomorrow."

The king extolled the young man's intelligence, remarked on his bravery, and commended his courage. "Metse-Tsate-Nfo is as an example for the young. He is the future of a great people," the king intoned. "One day, in the not-so-distant future, Metse-Tsate-Nfo will join the ranks of the Unknowable," Atabe concluded. Sense-Pass-King knelt on one knee and thanked Nfo Atabe for paying him this public homage. He declared himself unworthy of such encomiums. He promised to be a good role model for the nation's youth. He walked majestically to the throne and sat down. No sooner did his buttocks touch the *ndip* than the chair collapsed. He fell down the hole to the bottom of the pit. The king's *ntsendia* jumped to their feet, ululating like women, and immediately went to work throwing stones, spears, sticks into the pit. Such foolish men! What is a king worth without his sycophants? Metse-Tsate-Nfo was long gone. Once the chair hit the floor of the pit, Sense-Pass-King made for the secret passage and ran all the way to his house.

When day broke the following morning, Sense-Pass-King was seen sitting in front of his mother's house, sucking on his pipe. It is said that the king fainted when the *ntsendia* confirmed the story. Nfo Atabe was forced to abdicate and Metse-Tsate-Nfo was crowned as the new king.

The story is finished.

The Man-Eating Lion

There once lived a palm nut cutter. He had one wife and one child, a girl. The man dearly loved his daughter and often took her with him on short visits within the village. He sometimes let her carry his raffia bag, slung across her chest as if she were a boy. But harvesting palm nuts often kept him away from home during the day. When the man left home in search of palm trees laden with ripe fruits, the daughter would burst into tears, she'd run after him, she'd beg to go with him.

"My mother,[1] you can't come with me to the forest," her father repeatedly told her. "You're too young to accompany me to the forest. Besides, there's terror in the forest. The eye that sees the lion flees from it."

She was not consoled by his warnings. Every day she wept and every day her father refused to take her with him. One day, she secretly followed him. The man climbed a palm tree, harvested a cluster of nuts, and just as he turned around to throw the bunch down he saw his daughter standing under the tree. Had he not been vigilant, he would have thrown the cluster directly on her head. He flung the cluster farther away, climbed down the tree, and took his daughter home.

The palm nut cutter was very worried about his daughter's behavior, for it was common knowledge that a man-eating lion

[1]Affectionate usage; this daughter might also be named after her paternal grandmother.

lived in the woods on the outskirts of the village. The lion was known to sneak into the village and capture children for its food. It hunted adults only when there were no children on the playgrounds. The people beseeched their chief to send men into the forest to hunt the lion, but the chief was afraid of losing more men and refused. The lion kept on killing children. It soon began attacking women, but the chief would not change his mind.

This was the heart of the harvest season, and the palm nut cutter made the difficult decision to spend two weeks at home watching over his family. After that fortnight he got restless and went out in search of nuts. He was worried that the palm nuts would rot and he'd lose a good crop. Again, his daughter secretly followed him, but once in the forest she lost sight of him. She searched for her father. She went from tree to tree, looked under one thicket after another, followed one track and another, but couldn't find her father. After roaming the forest for half a day she came face to face with the lion. The lion captured her and carried her off to a secret spot deep inside the forest. At that special spot, the lion removed a plant cluster to reveal a well-camouflaged hole. The hole opened the way down a path into his house. He pushed the girl down the hole and followed after her. Once inside, the lion covered the hole with the plant.

Lion's house was built entirely of human bones. It comprised seven rooms. Lion dragged the girl to the last room. He poured palm oil in a pot large enough to hold three tins of oil. He put the pot on the hearth, lit a fire, and went to sleep. The little girl watched the oil slowly come to a boil and pondered her escape from Lion's ossuary. Though frightened, she kept very quiet and remained calm. She had to make every effort to stay awake. What had her father said? "The eye that sees a lion flees from it." She had got herself into this trouble; she was going to get herself out of it. She waited for Lion to go to sleep and then she waited until she could hear his snore rattle the bones along the walls. She tiptoed out of the room. One by one, she opened the doors, stepped through, and closed each door after her. When she got to the fourth door, she fashioned a piece of stick as tall as herself. She sharpened one end of the stick and planted the other end in the ground. She then opened but did not close the last three doors. She ran down the path to the hole, punched out the plant Lion had used to disguise the entrance of the hole, lifted herself out, and carefully closed the hole. She ran and didn't stop until she got home to her parents.

Lion woke up and could not find the girl in the room. "My god! My meat has escaped. My meat has disappeared. Well, where can it go? How far can it get? I'll follow and overtake the thing on the way," Lion snarled at the pot of boiling oil.

He opened the door. The girl was not in the room. He angrily threw open the second door, sniffed the air, and rushed through the third door. The girl was nowhere in sight. In a blind rage, he threw all his weight at the next door. He was confronted in the fourth room by a piece of stick the size and height of the young girl. A thunderous growl ripped through the room, as Lion pulled himself upright, and pounced on what he thought was his prisoner. The sharp end of the stick went through his heart and out through his back. Lion groaned as he let out his last breath, cursing the little human.

Safely back at home, the girl told her parents about what she had done. Her father summoned all the courage he could muster, loaded his Dane gun, and asked his daughter to take him to this secret hole. The daughter led the way to Lion's underground seven-room house, where the father confirmed Lion's death. He rushed to the palace and informed the chief.

"My child, the one who went missing, the one I thought the lion had eaten, has come back. She killed the wild beast that has been terrorizing us. Our chief should send men to go carry the animal."

"What you are telling me is a lie," the chief chastised him. "You know the penalty for lying to your chief about something this important."

"Mbeh, the punishment is death."

The chief stubbornly maintained the father was lying. The people began to question their chief's leadership. They were now skeptical of his motives: "This child was missing. For seven days we mourned her death. Now you say she is a liar? Where could the girl be hiding for a week or even two weeks and not be spotted? Mbeh can only be a king because of his people. You know that when a madman walks naked it is his kinsmen who feel ashamed. This little girl was brave enough to save all of us. All we ask of you is to be our chief and send your *ntsendia* to verify whether this child is telling the truth."

Humiliated, the chief had to blow his horn. All the villagers flocked to the palace. They followed the man and his daughter to the hole in the forest. The girl removed the plant, entered the hole, and led the way into Lion's den. She took them to the last room where they could see the boiling pot of palm oil for themselves. They carried the lion back to the village where it was slaughtered and the meat shared among the villagers. The head and the lion's skin were sent to the palace as custom demanded.

The story is finished.

The Flutes

This story was passed down to me by my mother, who heard it from her mother. I learned to play the flute because of the boys in this story.

"Are you listening?"

"Yes."

"Are you?"

"Yes, we are."

"I will proceed, then."

A man had two wives.[1] Each wife bore him four children. As the family size increased, the family had to trek miles and miles, farther and farther away from the village every year, to find arable land. Consequently, the women owned farms far, far away from home. One year they farmed at Akontom; three years later, they farmed at Ntah Metse.[2] One woman even cultivated her cocoyam farm as far away as Mbe-amfi.[3] This was

[1]The practice of polygamy used to be a fact of life among the Beba right through the mid-twentieth century. A lot has changed since with the advent of education and especially rural exodus. The fon of Beba still has many wives, his and those he inherited from his father. However, polygamous marriage is less common in today's Beba society.

[2]The original settlement site of the Beba. See also the discussion of migration and settlement of the Beba in the Afterword.

[3]*Mbe* meaning forest, *amfi* meaning dark; dark forest, implying land with fertile soil.

hard on the family, for they had to ascend and descend at least seven hills before they reached any of these farms—not to mention that crossing rivers was treacherous at the height of the rainy and harvest season.

One day, when they left for one of the farms, a son of the first wife took his flute with him. They toiled all day on the farm and the boy forgot his flute when they left at sunset.

"I cannot sleep if I do not go and get my flute," the boy told his mother, father, and stepmother.

"No! It's already dark," they said.

"I must go for it."

"You can't. That farm has ghosts. Why do you insist on going there tonight? Can't you collect it tomorrow when we go back to the farm?"

The boy was adamant. "I must go for my flute!"

"You know what happened to the boy who disobeyed his parents, don't you?"

The boy's parents recounted scary stories about what befell disobedient children, but they could not shake his resolve. Seeing his determination, they let him go. After all, isn't it said that if you put your hand in fire and the fire burns you, you should not complain? They thought their son was behaving like the chirping cricket that invites its own death. The boy threw all caution to the wind and walked in darkness to the farm. He searched and searched for the flute but couldn't find it. He was about to give up when he saw some ghosts sitting in a group and conversing. They were the strangest-looking people he had ever seen. Worse, they talked through their noses.

"Why are you here? What has brought you here?" one of them snorted.

"This is our farm. I have come for my flute. I forgot it here earlier today," the boy replied.

"Well, son, this is our home. Your family visits it during the day, so you think it belongs to you, but all this is ours. If you see the flute will you know it? Can you recognize your flute if we show it to you?"

"Yes, I can. It is a bamboo flute. It is brown and old. I made it myself. Just bring the one that belongs to me and I will recognize it."

The ghosts took the boy into a house. They brought out one flute. It shone so bright one would think the sun had forgotten to close its eyelids. The boy took one look at it and said no. They brought another one, the color of a king's gold. The boy shook his head and said, "Please, bring only my flute." They put his flute among shiny flutes and showed all these brightly colored flutes to the boy. They wanted the brightness to deceive him, but the boy pushed them aside and finally picked a wooden one.

"Is that the flute?"

"Yes, it is."

"Are you sure this is the flute you were playing with today?"

"I am certain it is the one."

"Play it."

The boy put the flute to his lips.

Father and Mother-Mine
Warned me not to come here
That it was too dark to go so far
I did not listen
Father and Mother-Mine
Warned me about the ghosts
I did not listen

The ghosts listened to the boy's song. They conferred and concurred that he was a hard nut to crack. They told the boy the flute test was over. They showed him to a room and told him to take whatever he wanted. The boy entered the room, where he saw many things, such things people yearn for every day. He came back and told them he had scrutinized all the things in the room but found nothing in the house as valuable as his flute. They tried a second time.

"Nothing here catches my eye. Nothing here is as valuable as this flute that brought me here."

They took him to another room full of pots of all sizes.

"What gift then can we give you for having come right to our home?"

"I don't want anything," the boy replied.

"Nonsense," they said. "Where have you ever heard of a guest going home empty-handed after a visit? Please, take whatever pot you want."

The boy looked at the pots and took the smallest one.

"There are big pots in there. Why do you prefer this small one? Why don't you take a big pot to your mother so that she can use it for her cooking? What can you put inside this thing? You can't even use it for cooking soup."

"This is the one that I like. There is none other that catches my eye in there. I cannot take any other pot. I would sooner go home without it, because I came here for my flute and nothing else."

"Never come here again," they warned. "On your way home, when you hear *gwran, gwran, gwran,* jump into the bushes. When you hear *tip, tip, tip,* come out of the bushes and continue your journey."

The boy thanked the ghosts and left. On the way home, when he heard *gwran, gwran, gwran,* he jumped into the bushes. When he heard *tip, tip, tip,* he jumped out and continued walking. The ghosts treated him this way until they escorted him home. His parents were relieved to see him.

"Have you returned?" they greeted in unison.

"Yes, I have returned."

They wondered out loud whether he had a headache. The father was afraid his son might be ill because of his encounter with the ghosts. He put some *afuondo*[4] in his palm, mixed it with palm oil, and gave it to his son, but the boy refused to take it.

"I do not want any *afuondo.* Don't touch me with any medicine. I am all right."

The parents couldn't shake their anxiety all night. They were worried the ghosts he had encountered were bad spirits, the type of ghosts that might have *passed over* their son. If that were the case, their son was as good as dead. But the boy slept peacefully through the night to the break of a new day. The boy's mother prepared the morning meal and they all sat down and ate. The boy then gave the pot he had brought with him to his father. The father opened it and things kept pouring out of the pot, filling up the entire house. Some people quickly ran out of the house; others could hardly walk around the bounty. The father slowly overcame his surprise and thanked his ancestors. The ghosts had been good ancestral spirits after all. Reassured, he then shared all the riches among his wives, children, and relatives. He also gave to their neighbors and the visitors who had spent the night in the compound. His task completed, they gathered their farm tools and prepared to leave for another day of work.

"Did you put your flute in your bag?" the second wife asked her own son.

"No," the boy replied.

The woman said, "People carry flutes in their bags, and those flutes bring them good things, don't you see it? Now you have left the house without your flute. Can't you take yours so it can bring more things for your mother? Won't you be happy about

[4]All-powerful Beba medicine—*afu* means medicine, *ndo* means horn—a panacea, preserved in a small horn, usually given to people for protection of any kind and especially from evil spirits and poison. If a child eats something that could be harmful, the child is automatically given *afuondo* before any other treatment is administered.

that?" she asked her son, and beat him. "Go back. Take your flute and put it in your bag!"

The boy refused to go for the flute. It is said that greed blinded this woman's heart and she furiously beat her son. They say she beat him and beat him repeatedly; she beat him so badly she split his head open. She stopped only when she saw his blood. The wounded child ran to the house, took his flute, and joined the rest of the family. They trekked to the farm and worked all day. When evening came and it was time to go home, the boy put his flute in his bag. His mother saw what he'd done and beat him again.

"Leave your flute in the farm," she angrily ordered her son. "Don't you know how to forget a flute?"

The boy was afraid, as darkness was already approaching. He removed the flute from his bag and tossed it into the farm. They got home, and the woman didn't bother to go to the river with the others for a refreshing bath. She quickly cooked the evening meal, and they all sat down to eat. The woman kept looking anxiously at her son while he ate. The boy had hardly finished his meal when she said, "Aren't you going to get your flute?"

The boy said, "I will not go to that farm. I wanted to bring my flute home and you asked me to leave it there. That farm is a farm of ghosts. I will not go there at night."

"If you don't go, I will kill you. If that happens, we cannot sleep in this house or live in this village anymore."

She picked up her cane and beat her son. The boy was more terrified at the thought of banishment from the village. He left, crying all the way to the farm. As soon as he saw the group of ghosts, he walked up to them.

"What have you come here for?" the ghosts asked him, speaking through their noses.

"We were coming to the farm this morning. Mother said I should put my flute in my bag. I put it in and brought it here. We were going back this evening. Mother said I should leave my flute in the farm. I left it here. She has said I should come and get it."

"If you see your flute, will you recognize it?"

"Yes."

They took him to the house, showed him the room of flutes, and said to him, "Take the flute that is your own." There were golden flutes, silver flutes, brass flutes, all handcrafted, all alluring. As soon as the boy saw the most beautifully decorated flute, he pounced on it and said, "This is my flute."

"Is that the one?"

The boy said, "Yes."

"Are you sure?"

"Don't you think I know my own flute?"

"Play it for us, then."

The boy inhaled and blew into the flute. The ghosts listened to his song.

um um um these ghosts smell
um um um these ghosts smell

"Put it in your bag," the noses snorted when he finished.

Next, they showed him to the room full of pots. When the boy entered the room, he saw an array of pots: big ones and small ones, red pots, brown pots, green pots; pots of all shapes and sizes. He thought, If I take a big one a lot more things will come out of it. Without hesitation, he took the biggest one.

The noses hummed at him, "From today, never come here again. On your way back home, if you hear *gwran, gwran, gwran,* jump into the bushes. If you hear *tip, tip, tip,* step out of the bushes and continue your journey."

The boy immediately took leave of the ghosts. He had not walked a considerable distance when he heard *gwran, gwran, gwran.* He hurried along and when he heard *tip, tip, tip,* he jumped into the bushes. That's what happened between the boy and the ghosts until they drove him into the compound.

The boy knocked on his mother's door. She threw open the door, took the pot, and hid in the darkest corner of her house.

"You see. I said it was a simple thing. Many things came out of that small pot. What will I do with the things that will come out of this one?"

She locked the door and they went to sleep. The following morning, she cooked food and, ancestors forbid, she ate with her children behind closed doors.[5] She then took the pot from the dark corner and opened it. Illnesses came out of the pot and killed them all. The sun shone bright over the hills, but the woman's door remained shut. Her husband wondered why the woman and her children were still asleep. He went and knocked on the door. There was no answer.

"They spent the night here. If they had left early for the farm, wouldn't someone have heard them leave?"

He knocked again and still there was no reply. He forced open the door. A small quantity of diseases escaped. Sensing that something terrible had happened, the man quickly shut the door. It is said that all the diseases that we have on earth, such as measles, chickenpox, cholera, diarrhoea, malaria, yellow fever, epilepsy, sleeping sickness, leprosy, all came out of that house when the concerned husband opened that door. Had he not quickly shut that door, there would be more diseases, more illnesses, and more plagues than those that exist on our earth today.

The story is finished.

[5]Eating in broad daylight behind closed doors is considered the sign of utmost selfishness. One is always expected to share food with those in the home and with passersby even though passersby might stop just for a moment to extend a greeting before moving on. The implied expectation is that they should be given the opportunity to turn one's generosity down. Eating behind closed doors in the daytime is therefore construed as greedy and as antisocial behavior that can be seen as or result in a curse on the family. See the story "When You Eat Today, Remember There Is Tomorrow."

The Boy and the Dish

A long time ago, there lived another man who also had two wives. The first wife had a son. The second wife was also blessed, for she too had a son. But the first wife did not live to see old age. She died suddenly from one of those mysterious illnesses people often succumbed to and no one, not a healer, not a diviner, can say exactly what killed them. Her family grieved for her. The death celebrations over, her son was left in the care of her co-wife.

But this co-wife was not a kind woman. She was called the-wicked-one because she didn't treat the little boy as her own. People talked, but she didn't care that custom and tradition demanded this of her. It was considered shameful if one visited a compound and could tell which children belonged to which mother by the way they were treated. It was clear by her attitude that this boy could never be her son. He remained a stepson to her. People said she treated him as if he were a leper. She sent him to the farm to weed grass, to harvest food; she sent him to the forest to fetch firewood; at home, she made him do all the housework. Her son spent all his time at home eating, sleeping, and playing. You'd never see him doing any of the chores: he would not wash a dish, he would not sweep the floor, he would not go to the river like any other child and wash his own clothes. His mother worshipped him like a god, and he took his brother for his slave.

It all happened one day when the boy came back from the farm exhausted and famished. Rather than give the boy food to eat, the stepmother ordered him to carry the dirty dishes to the stream. Knowing what any form of protest could provoke, the boy obediently carried the basin full of dirty dishes to the stream in spite of his fatigue and the hunger gnawing at his ribs. It was the rainy season. The water was cold, but he carefully washed and rinsed dish after dish. While he was busy loading the clean dishes into the silver basin, one of the bowls fell from his hands and was swept away by the strong current. The stepmother was furious when the boy came home without the dish and promptly ordered him to go and look for it. The boy begged and pleaded with her; he complained that night was fast approaching, but she took no pity on him. She wanted her dish, be it night or day.

"Do not return without it," she decreed.

Weeping bitterly and thinking about his mother, the boy called upon the dead woman to come to his aid. He left the house, the fear in the balls of his feet propelling his steps as he ran all the way to the stream. He searched the waters for a long time. The more he waded downstream, the higher the water rose, to his knees, his thighs, and his chest. Slowly but surely the waters engulfed him. To his surprise, instead of drowning, he saw a path in front of him. He took the path and it led him to a single house in front of which was sitting an old, old woman. He felt a knot in his stomach, fought down his apprehension, approached the old woman, and greeted her.

"Grandmother, are you at home?"

"Welcome, my son."

"Is all well with you?"

"I'm all right, but you, where are you going to this hour of the day?"

The boy sat down and told the old woman the story of the missing dish: "My mother sent me to the stream to wash our dishes. One of them was swept away and I came downstream looking for it. My search led me to your house. Mi,[1] have you seen our bowl?"

She listened and at the end of the story she asked the boy to spend the night with her. She could see he was hungry and asked him to cook some food for both of them.

"Go behind the house. You'll find a bunch of plantain. Pluck some, peel the plantain, but cook the peelings," the old woman instructed.

The boy did as he was told. When the peels cooked they turned into real plantains. Grandmother then instructed him to go to the chicken house, to scrape together some chicken droppings, and to fry them. The boy saw many eggs in the pen. He dutifully collected some droppings, which he beat together and fried in palm oil. The fried batter turned into an omelette. The boy and the old woman ate their fill and went to sleep.

The following day, the old woman asked the boy to go to the chicken house and pick an egg that was as black as dirt. The boy picked the dirty egg. Grandmother then gave him the dish. "Give it to your mother but break the egg in front of your father's house," she instructed. The boy thanked her and followed the path leading away from her house. He walked and walked for what felt like a day, thinking he might never get home again. But just as suddenly, he found himself under water and he waded upstream to the pool where he usually came to wash dishes. He got home, gave the dish to his stepmother, and broke the egg in front of his father's house. All the wealth one can wish for poured out of that egg: money, cars, bicycles, paved roads, houses flooded with electricity and pipe-borne water—all the comfort the boy could never have imagined. When the boy's father heard his story, he embraced his son and warmly congratulated him.

[1]Respectful form of address, meaning Mother.

The stepmother saw all this and envy burned in her heart. She wanted to own wealth, more wealth than this boy had found. She immediately called her son and gave him dishes to wash at the stream. The son pouted and threw a tantrum. The mother stood her ground. The son flew into a rage and grumbled all day but could not bend his mother's will. He had to take the dishes to the stream, where he spent the entire afternoon. At last he returned with all the dishes, but his chest, arms, and hands were all stained with soot and palm oil. He had no knowledge of using sand and *awawa*[2] leaves to wash dirty pots. The mother ignored the pots and berated her son.

"Can't you lose a dish? Go back and throw this dish into the river," she commanded.

The son obeyed. But when evening came she ordered the boy to go find her dish. The son complained that it was getting dark. He complained that the dish must have been carried far, far away by the current, but his mother would hear none of it. She called him a spoiled brat and threatened his life. The boy left for the stream. Halfway downstream he was swallowed up by the water. He followed the same path as his brother and soon found himself in front of the old woman's house. Without a word of greeting, he addressed her.

"Old woman, my mother has asked me to come and look for her dish. Have you seen it anywhere?"

"I know where it is, but you'll have to spend the night here and go back tomorrow."

"I don't want to spend the night here."

Grandmother ignored him. Rather, she asked the boy to cook some plantain peelings and fry some fowl droppings for their evening meal. Something must be wrong with this old woman's head, the boy snickered. He cooked the plantains and fried the eggs instead. The plantains turned into peelings and the egg

[2] *Awawa* leaves feel like sandpaper to the touch.

batter into fowl droppings. They both went to bed hungry. In the morning, the old woman asked the boy to go to the chicken house and take an egg black with dirt. The boy took an egg that shone like the early dry-season moon. The old woman gave him the dish and bade him good-bye. He went away without saying a word of thanks.

As soon as his mother saw him, she rushed to the boy and seized the egg. She was overjoyed, for she knew that a shiny egg was full of more promises than a dirty one. She took her son far away into the forest and broke the egg only when she was sure they were alone. It is said that a masquerade of evil spirits came out of that shiny egg and clubbed them to death. The things jealousy can make us do! Wickedness and lust for wealth led the evil stepmother and her son to their deaths. That is why our people still tell stories and sing songs about the jealous stepmother today.

The story is finished.

The Unhappy Stepson

A woman died, leaving her only child with her husband. She surrendered to the wrath of the gods the year of the great floods. Her husband later married another wife. She had five sons and completely forgot about her stepson. Worse, this woman always put food for her sons in clean pans but made her stepson use a *nkenkap* leaf.[1] This went on through adolescence and well into manhood. Soon, the boys had to build their own houses, marry, and take care of their own families.

It so happened that the daughter of the chief did not want to marry any of the men who desired the princess. Her father grew worried with each passing year and so, he began a tradition in honor of his daughter. Every year, he threw a feast, hoping the princess would fall in love and choose one of the men who thronged to the palace. As you can imagine, the stepmother looked forward to this annual bonanza. On each occasion, she methodically cleaned her sons, dressed them in expensive *tob*, and took them to the feast. She'd mix a full basket of beans with a bucket of sand and ask her stepson to sort out the beans in their absence. She'd instruct him to finish the task by their return. This went on for years.

[1]The *nkenkap* is a creeper that grows in the forest. The leaves look like plantain leaves but are much smaller and of a tougher texture. Plantain leaves are the more commonly used to serve or preserve food. The Beba do not use *nkenkap* leaves to serve food. However, raw food can be wrapped and cooked in *nkenkap* leaves.

The year of our story, the boy was left to his usual task. Have you ever felt the pain when a grain of sand is caught between your teeth when you're chewing cooked rice? That's how miserable the boy felt as he performed this task. In deep pain he stood up and stepped away from the basket. He walked to the edge of the *nsaa* where his mother was buried and wept at her grave.

"Why did you die and leave me behind to be mistreated? You'd better take me with you," he moaned, his tears falling on his mother's grave.

When his tears touched the earth, the grave opened up and the mother emerged.

"What's wrong?" she asked. "It's not your time yet. Why are you here?"

"Mother, take me with you. I can't live with my brothers and stepmother anymore."

The boy cried and recounted the problems he had faced since her death. She listened and shoveled all the beans into a tin. She washed him clean and applied some palm kernel oil to his body. His skin shone with the handsomeness of a rainy-season full moon. She outfitted him with a finely embroidered *njumpa* and gave him a horse. The boy mounted and rode to the palace. The courtyard was swarming with people. He had never seen so many people at one gathering. Although the boy was intimidated by this crowd, he kept on riding. From her elevated seat, the princess watched his approach. Her eyes never left him. They remained fixed on the young rider and his horse. When the rider drew nearer the princess smacked her lips and told her father that her husband had arrived.

"Really?" the stunned father asked. "Where is he?"

"There he is, coming right there, perched on top of that horse."

The young man approached, dismounted, and entered the arena of festivities. The princess stepped down from the throne her father had built specially for her and fell on the young man.

"This is my husband. This is my husband."

Startled, the boy slipped out of her hands and fled. One of his shoes fell to the ground when he struggled to mount his horse. He didn't stop for it. He rode back with one shoe to his mother's grave. The clothes he wore disappeared along with the horse into the grave. He went back to work on the tin of beans.

People searched for the boy everywhere, but they couldn't find him. The princess cried night and day. She was broken-hearted. The chief sent his messengers, the *ntsendia,* out into the village with the boy's shoe. He decreed that all the boys living in the village had to try on the shoe. The *ntsendia* scoured the village, but the shoe would not fit any of the young men whose compounds they visited. When they arrived at the boy's compound, the stepmother kept him in a dark corner of the house. First, she presented her oldest son to the *ntsendia.* He tried on the shoe. The boy's foot was too big. The mother immediately took a knife and pruned away part of her son's foot. When he tried on the shoe a second time, the foot was too small. Eventually, all her sons failed the test.

"Are these all the male children in this compound?" the *ntsendia* asked the woman.

The woman pointed at her stepson crouching in the corner. "I don't know whether that one can put his foot in the royal shoe," she stammered.

The *ntsendia* called for the boy. He hesitated but they beckoned him to come forward. He barely stuck his toes in and the shoe engulfed his foot. The woman was startled. Before she knew it she exclaimed, "This filthy child? Might that person who came to the palace the other day be this nasty, miserable thing?" She was bitter, bitter in the throat.

The boy and the shoe were taken to the palace. The chief welcomed him and gave him food and shelter. But the boy didn't feel at home at the palace and soon got restless. One day, when most people had gone away to their farms, the boy sneaked away to his mother's grave and implored her: "Mother, I am here."

The grave opened up and the mother emerged. She got him dressed exactly as she had the first time. She gave him a ring.

"When you go back today, tell the chief you want to take your wife away with you. Leave this village and look for land beyond those hills. You will cross seven rivers to get there. This ring will help you start a new life with your wife."

The boy went back to the palace and straight to the chief's chamber.

"Mbeh, I think my wife and I can now find a place of our own."

"Well, son, what becomes the fate of the pot will also be that of the cocoyam. I don't think my daughter will object. Since your wife loves you, you can go where you like. Come and visit us soon enough."

The boy and his wife said their good-byes. They rode for days until they left the borders of their hilly village behind them and arrived at an open plain.

"Do you like this place?"

"I can breathe the air," she teased.

Night was already approaching. He harnessed the horse and left his wife sitting under a tree. He went about the bushes and gathered some twigs and wood. He made a fire and they basked in its warmth. His drowsy wife soon fell asleep under the tree. He waited until she was deeply asleep, stood up, and walked away from her. He spoke to the ring. A fenced compound with giant houses appeared in the area next to the tree.

"Wake up, my princess. Let's go home," he said, gently tapping her left shoulder.

She woke up and looked around with sleepy eyes but did not see a house. He took her hand and led her to the house and, the people say, to happiness.

"Do you see? That is our compound. This is our house."

She smiled and opened the door, and he stepped in behind her.

The story is finished.

The Disobedient Son

It was the beginning of the dry season. It was that time of the year when the last *achu*-cocoyams were dug out of the ground before the land was prepared for the new planting season. That morning the woman in our story took three of her children with her to the farm for such a harvest. When they arrived at the farm, they saw a man digging up some of their cocoyams. This man had dirty long fingernails, long pointed teeth, a bald head, and a very long beard. She greeted the man, who responded in an old raspy voice. She immediately recognized him for what he was: a spirit in human form; a ghost, not a good one but one of those bad ghosts, the offspring of ogres. She engaged him in conversation.

"Father, did your day break?"

"Yes, my daughter. And yours?"

"We are well. We've just come here for some food. And you?"

"I am hungry and since I have no one to take care of me, I've come to harvest some cocoyams."

"You don't have a wife?"

"No."

"You don't have children?"

"No."

"No brothers? Uncles? Sisters? . . ."

"No, I don't have any family."

"Is that why you've kept such a long beard?"

"I don't own a pair of scissors," he grunted.

"I can be of help."

The woman had barely finished her sentence when a flash of lightning ripped across the sky. Dark clouds swirled overhead, violent winds spanked the trees, and the rain came in long slashes. The downpour nurtured a storm punctuated by thunderclap after thunderclap.

"I live over there." The bearded figure raised a gnarled finger and pointed at a house in the distance. "You can take shelter and wait out the rain," he offered.

The woman and her children gladly accepted his offer and followed him to the house. The more they walked, the heavier the rain and the further away the house seemed to be. They could see wisps of smoke spiraling through the thatched roof as they got closer to the house. He led them into a smoke-filled room. The woman and her children sat down and the bearded man fed the fire. They sat comfortably close to the hearth, where the flames were warm and somnific. The heat dried their clothes and soon absorbed the chill. The longer the wood fire burned, the more the smoke cleared. Only then did the woman look around the room. Behind the bearded man's mud-bed were rows of human skulls. She looked at her children and was struck by an idea. She called her son to her side and mumbled under her breath, "Go home and don't come back." Then aloud she said, "Go to the house and bring the pair of scissors I put on the windowsill in your father's house."

Mandiengoh refused to go. He sat down and moved even closer to the golden embers. The mother called her oldest daughter and, raising her voice, told her to go and get the scissors. Before the daughter left the house the mother whispered, "Go and don't come back." Atah took the hint, went home, and did not return. In the meantime, the woman and her second daughter worked on kindling the fire. The mother would add more firewood, and the daughter would kneel and blow on the embers until the flames exploded, engulfing the wood. After a considerable lapse of time, the woman sighed and exclaimed, "Maweghndia, I don't know why your sister hasn't come back with the pair of scissors yet. Go and see what is happening and be quick about it." Maweghndia went home but did not return. The woman turned again to her son.

"Go and see why your sisters are taking so long," she pleaded.

The boy again ignored his mother.

"Oh, children these days . . . I am going to see what those two girls are up to," she told the bearded figure. "They will be sorry they've disobeyed me," she said and left the man's house.

When evening came, the ghost left his house and the curious boy hid himself under the mud-bed. The ghost went and invited his brethren to his house. When the ghost returned, he got hold of Mandiengoh and chopped off his head. He made excellent soup for their cocoyams. His head found a place among the row of human skulls behind the mud-bed.

The story is finished.

The Two Sisters

Tachi Nanga was known the world over because no one could match his dexterity at making drums. He could stretch animal hide to the exact pitch so skillfully that people came from far and wide, traveling for days, sometimes months, to place their orders or simply watch him work the hide. They say it was like magic. His fingers handled the hide the same way a diviner's palm coaxes cowries or kola nut halves for their messages. But the two sisters whose lives were changed by Tachi Nanga knew nothing about his fame as a drum maker and drummer. It was rather his buttocks that endeared him to the girls.

These girls had lost their mother when they were quite young. She died giving birth to the third child, who was unfortunately stillborn. The girls were neglected by their relatives, and although their father remarried, things did not change with their new mother. They felt like orphans and alone in the world. They were often sent to the farm, where they were made to toil all day, and when they returned home had nothing or very little to eat. They complained, but their father would not come to their rescue.

One day, the older daughter made a drastic decision. She cooked food for herself, packed all of it in a *neshre*,[1] and left the

[1]Plural, *meshre.* A container made of cane, used mainly by women, to transport things to and harvested foods from the farm. It can be used to carry anything. Men do not carry *meshre* (although young

compound. She did not know where she was going. Not that it mattered to her. She remembered the saying that a road will lead you to another road and another road and another, so she kept on walking. Passersby who questioned her got the same answer: "I am not going anywhere."

She walked for a day, through the night and yet another day. and finally arrived at the banks of a river. The hairs stood erect on her arms, for the river was as dark as night. She walked cautiously toward the river and as she approached it, she saw an old woman, older than anyone she had ever seen in her life. The woman was so old her back was completely bent. She was sitting near the river, her head between her thighs, her left hand in a dark pool of water. The girl hesitated, shifted the *neshre* on her back, and walked up to the old woman. The old woman lifted her head very slowly, squinted at the girl, and put her head back between her thighs. The girl walked past her, leaned her *neshre* against a rock, took in a deep breath, and swung the *neshre* from her back and around onto her thigh. She then lifted the *neshre* from her thigh to the ground, tipped it against the rock, and walked back to the old woman.

"Mother, my greetings to you."

"What's your name, my child?"

"Grandmother, my name is Manda."

"Where are you from? What brings you here, my child?"

"I'm only wandering about, Mother. I don't know why."

"I've been sitting here for a long time with nothing to eat. Do you have any food in your *neshre?*"

boys do)—men use bags or sacks that they carry over their shoulders or they use *bendjob* (see the story "King-of-Scabies"). Because the *neshre* is carried on the back, the part that lies on the back is flat and the rest of the container has a widening semicircle-like oval shape that opens out from the flat side, up, and around. A specially woven belt, about two inches wide, known as a *tou* is used to carry the *neshre.* When carrying a *neshre,* the *tou* runs from the back of the *neshre,* up by the ears, to the woman's forehead and is adjusted for comfort.

Manda removed four bundles of *achu* and a cup of soup and gave the food to the old woman. She thanked Manda and quietly ate her fill. Manda made a funnel out of a plantain leaf, carried water from the river, and gave it to the old woman.

"You've saved me from the pangs of death. I was sitting here because I was very hungry and had no strength in my legs. May the ancestors be with you as you continue on your journey. When you go a distance you'll come to a place with two paths. If you see one that has been cleaned and it shines with brightness, ignore it. If you see the one overgrown with grass, take it. Do you hear me?"

"Yes, mother," she replied. "But you are only saying this to me. What will happen to you? I don't want to leave you here alone."

"Don't worry. Go ahead. I'll be right behind you."

Manda carried her *neshre* and continued walking until she came upon a path that was as clean as a road used by cars. She also saw a path overgrown with tall grass. She ignored the path the old woman had forbidden her to take and followed the grassy path. She had not walked a kilometer when to her surprise she found herself on a wide paved road. She followed it and arrived at a compound.

The man, Tachi Nanga, who lived there was a reputed drummer and drum maker. There are two things that Tachi Nanga could not live without: his drum and his cock. These were his faithful companions. Some men have wives and children, Tachi Nanga had his drum and his rooster. This cock was said to be like the whiteman's book. He was the repository of all the goings-on in the land and surrounding villages. He shared his wealth of knowledge with his master, Tachi Nanga. That day, before Tachi Nanga left for a death celebration, he instructed Cock to alert him if anything happened in his absence or if anyone came to the compound. Cock was standing outside when he saw a girl arrive with a big *neshre* on her back. He immediately crowed, calling on his master.

Tachi Nanga oh kong
nger wambu wambu wamo ze ma fe detso le kong
Tachi Nanga eh kong
A hideous newlywed has come here today ee kong

Manda was so exhausted she paid no heed to Cock's song. She was relieved to put down her *neshre* and rest her aching feet. She sat down inside the house and instantly fell asleep. As soon as Tachi Nanga heard Cock calling for him he climbed down from the drum he was beating, undid the rope that fastened the drum to his waist, threw the big drum on the celebration ground, *kpwem!* and hurriedly made his way home. Manda woke to a surprise. She saw a man coming toward her. How strangely he moved on his buttocks! The man entered the house, greeted her with his buttocks, and asked her her name with his buttocks.

"What kind of food will you eat?" the buttocks asked.

"Whatever you have. I eat all kinds of food," she replied.

Tachi Nanga cooked some *sese* plantain with smoked deer meat which he seasoned with palm oil, salt, and *njanga*—crayfish. He cooked with his buttocks. He served the food with his buttocks.

After the meal, the buttocks asked Manda, "What type of bed do you sleep in?"

"I do not have a preference. I will sleep on the bed you give me."

He gave her an animal skin. Manda spread the skin on the floor and went to sleep. How was she to know that Tachi Nanga would create ants and let them loose on her? The ants attacked her mercilessly. She woke up scratching herself. She ran up and down all night in a frenzy.

"How was your rest last night?" those buttocks inquired the following morning.

"The house is marvelous. How I slept! I was afraid I wasn't going to be able to sleep in a strange house but nothing bothered me."

Hearing this, Tachi Nanga left her alone and went and cooked more food with his buttocks.

"Since you got here, whenever I ask you a question your answer is *anything*. Now tell me, what type of food do you really want to eat?"

"I'll eat whatever you've cooked."

"What kinds of dishes do you serve food in where you come from?"

"We use plantain leaves."

He put her food in a *nkenkap* leaf and she ate it. He went out, tapped palm wine with his buttocks, came back, and served her with his buttocks. She'd become so used to this man who did everything with his buttocks that it no longer felt strange being there with him and his faithful companion. She drank all the palm wine her stomach could hold and slumbered all day. However, she did not eat all the food Tachi Nanga served her. She would not eat without sharing with Cock, who always sat staring at her while she ate. She was amused by how strangely master and companion behaved. Tachi Nanga always showed concern. He always ascertained she'd had enough food to eat. Then he'd ask Cock whether she had shared her food with him and Cock would promptly reply, "No. That woman is a bad bad woman. Her greediness stinks." You have to agree that Cock behaved exactly like the mother hen that eats, wipes its beak on the ground, and stares blankly at her chicks.

"When will you be leaving us?" Tachi Nanga inquired.

"I shall be leaving the day after tomorrow. I would like to spend two more days here."

On the day of her departure Tachi Nanga went to his farm, harvested a bunch of plantains, carried it home, and peeled and cooked the plantains with a lot of smoked meat. He used some freshly smoked *njomne*,[2] the type a young man would use to

[2]This animal is popularly known in the Bamenda grasslands as the grass cutter—cutting-grass in Pidgin English.

prepare a meal for his future mother-in-law. While the plantains cooked he cut some plantain leaves and lined the inside of Manda's *neshre.* He then poured the entire contents of the pot into the *neshre.* He covered the food with more plantain leaves to keep it warm for a good length of time.

"Why haven't you put some of the food aside for yourselves?" Manda asked Tachi Nanga. "You've packed my *neshre* full. It will be too heavy a load for me to carry."

"Carry your *neshre* and be on your way," her host chided. "There's a lot of food in this house. Won't I be cooking some more?"

She thanked him, and as soon as he stepped out of the house, Manda removed some of the plantain and meat, filled a dish, and gave it to Cock. He devoured the food so fast that when his master asked whether he had tasted of the plantain he promptly said, "Not a piece," and whined about how hungry he was. Tachi Nanga left for his palm bush and Cock gave the girl the following instructions:

"As you return home, you will want to have a bath. If you see a pool that sparkles like a python's egg, leave it alone. Keep going until you see the one that is very dark. Do not be afraid. Step into its waters and refresh yourself."

Manda thanked Cock and left. On her way, she came to a sparkling pool and kept on walking. When she came upon a river with waters as dark as the one on whose banks she had met the old woman she stopped. She bit her lower lip, swung the *neshre* from her back down to her raised left thigh. She took a deep breath and slowly lifted the *neshre* from her thigh and placed it on the ground. She used a piece of stick as a wedge to anchor the bottom of the *neshre* to the earth. Her back ached from the trek and the weight of the food. Yes, on a long journey even a straw is heavy. Thoughts of the old woman flooded her mind as she removed her clothes and jumped into the pool. The water was cool and refreshing. She felt comforted and safe in its quiet serenity. She tarried in the water but the first batch of swallows and clockbirds zapped past her and disappeared downstream, taking with them the beautiful speculum on their wings reflected in the rays of the setting sun. She stepped out of the pool and was about to oil her skin when the old woman she had met before rose out of the water.

"Who is this?"

"I am the one," Manda replied.

"Where are you from?"

"I am only wandering about."

"Aren't you the child who passed here the other day?"

"I am," she answered.

"Are you going back?"

"Yes, Grandmother."

"Come here," the old woman beckoned.

Manda waded back into the pool and stood very still next to Grandmother. Grandmother lifted her wizened left hand and pointed, "Stand on this stone." Manda obeyed. Grandmother pushed her down into the dark waters. She disappeared into the deep for what seemed like an eternity. When she resurfaced she looked completely different. She was transformed into a very beautiful young woman gilded in expensive garments. Grandmother pushed her back into the pool. She received many trunks full of dresses. Grandmother pushed her down a third time. This time she received a baby and a baby-minder. They were both healthy, their hair coiffed, they wore earrings, and rows of *jigida* beads adorned their necks and waists. Grandmother pushed Manda into the pool one last time. She received a *mboneble mo.*[3]

"Did you bring any food with you?"

"Yes, Grandmother. There's a lot of food in my *neshre.*"

[3]A scrawny dog that eats the baby's poop; *neble*, meaning excrement; *mo* meaning a baby, a child.

Grandmother took some of the food, threw away the *neshre*, and gave her a new one. Manda put all her things inside. The old woman wished her a safe journey. Manda climbed seven hills, crossed rivers, descended seven hills, and finally arrived at their compound.

What a surprise! People didn't recognize this young woman. They had forgotten about Manda. When she arrived they were all stunned to discover who she was. They had all assumed she had run away and been killed by a wild animal. Her sister had mourned her. Even she did not recognize her own sister. Who was this woman? She was stunned to see her older sister so beautiful, returning home with a child, a baby-minder, a *mboneble mo*, and trunks full of things. She fell joyfully on Manda, pestering her with questions about her adventures, asking her where she had gone, where she was coming from.

"Why all these questions?" Manda asked, ignoring her younger sister. "Aren't you happy to see me?" she teased her sister. She removed two rows of *jigida* from her neck and put them around her sister's neck. She then removed three rows and gave them to her friend.

"I am your sister. Instead of giving three strings of beads to me and two to your friend, you give me two and three to your friend?" the younger sister protested. Manda gave her one more, bringing the number to three, and one more to her friend. Her sister was mortified.

"*I* am your sister. We come from the same womb. They say if you stand under a plum tree you'll eat ripe plums. You've gone on a journey; you've brought things . . . Why don't I deserve more? Why give me three strings of beads and four to your friend? Why not give me four and one or two to your friend?"

"Tegheh kwu! Dead-Father-of-Mine! You're right. Our people also say that the person standing under the tree is the one who knows what ants feed on. Go look for your own treasures and give me two rows of beads when you return!" Manda retorted.

I have to say our ancestors rightly warn us to beware what we name our children, for they quite often bear out the name. Ajientoh,[4] for that was the younger sister's name, sulked and in anger decided to leave their compound. She went and pounded some *achu*. It was the type of *achu* made by lazy women or by girls who never paid attention when their mothers cooked. Yes, Ajientoh's *achu* was very soft indeed, like a Bafut woman's *achu*. She put the bundles of soft *achu* in her *neshre*, carried the *neshre* on her back, and left the compound. She encountered many animals on the way. First, she came upon Nguh-the-Fowl, who inquired about her trip.

"Don't disturb my peace. Do you have to know where I am going?"

"I was only greeting you . . . You are such a pretty girl and I am so hungry," Nguh appealed to her vanity.

"Why should I care whether you are hungry? Are you in my house?"

She next crossed paths with Ankwunyab-the-Pig and instantly burst out, "Stop dirtying my way. How can I walk on such a dirty path?"

"Where are you off to?" Ankwunyab asked, ignoring her sharp tongue.

"Have pigs been asked to stand on the way and question people?"

"I was only extending you a word of greeting."

Then she met Bushi-the-Cat and sneered, "This skinny thing! Why are you scampering about so silently pretending you can't hurt a fly?"

"Please give me some food?" Bushi implored her.

"Have I been your feeder?" she snapped and kept on walking.

She came upon an old woman sitting on the banks of the river. This woman was so old and bent that her head rested between her thighs.

[4]Literally, one who eats and denies the fact; untrustworthy; a liar.

"Ndegheh kwu! Dead-Mother-of-Mine! What is this gaunt old thing sitting here for? Get out of my way quickly. I want to pass. Do not sit here and block my way."

The old woman stood up, moved one shaky step after another and made way for the girl.

"My daughter, where are you from and where are you going?"

"My God! Why is this old harridan bothering me? You may be old but you are not my mother. Who gave you permission to ask me questions?" She rolled her lips, spat, and put down her *neshre.* She undressed, jumped into the river, had a cool refreshing bath, and started off again.

"When you get to the clean path, do not follow it, keep to the grassy path instead," the old woman instructed her. Ajientoh arrived at the clean paved road, stood for a while, stared at it and left it alone. She followed the grassy path. As soon as she arrived at Tachi Nanga's *nsaa,* Cock came up to her. She promptly exclaimed, "What kind of a cock is this?"

Cock scampered back into the safety of the house. He sang, calling for his master.

Tachi Nanga oh kong
Tachi Nanga oh kong
nger wambu wambu wamo ze ma fe detso le kong
nger wambu wambu wamo ze ma fe detso le kong
Tachi Nanga eh kong
Tachi Nanga eh kong
A hideous newlywed has come here today ee kong
A hideous nger has come here today ee kong

Tachi Nanga heard him and immediately threw down the drum he was playing, *kpwem!* He hurried home, entering the house on his buttocks.

"Welcome. How was your journey? What will you eat?" he asked his guest.

"I eat only rice and fried meat."

Tachi Nanga cooked the meal she wanted.

"What type of dish would you like your food served in?"

"Do you have to ask? Do you imagine I eat in dirty pans or in a dog's pan?"

Tachi Nanga put the food in a clean dish. Ajientoh ate like a swarm of locusts ravaging a cassava farm. Cock put his head on the floor. He watched her while she ate. She did not give him a single grain of rice. As soon as she finished eating, she exploded with indignation, "What kind of a cock is this that puts its head on the floor, watching while people eat? Is this how the fowls of this village behave?" Cock looked pained. He stood up and slowly walked away to his master's side. Tachi Nanga had just returned from the farm and started cooking again with his buttocks. Ajientoh observed him closely and sighed. "What a pity!" she intoned. "Who's going to eat this buttock food?" she sighed again, watching Tachi Nanga dish out the food with his buttocks.

"Pity me! He is serving the food with his buttocks. Who is going to eat his buttock food?"

Tachi Nanga ignored her. No sooner had he put the cocoyam and beans in front of her than she gulped everything down. They all ate in silence and went to sleep. Later that night, Tachi Nanga created ants and filled the entire house with them. The ants tormented Ajientoh, and she screamed all through the night.

At dawn, Tachi greeted her, "Did you have a good night's sleep?"

"Weeh, if this is how people are supposed to sleep, then no one can sleep in this house of yours. In any case, I can't sleep here tonight. I am going back. Tegheh kwu! A house in which I can't sleep because ants bite so much! You gave me a bed. You claimed it was a white man's bed. Do ants ever bite people on a Vono bed? No. I am going away today. I can't sleep one more night in this house."

Tachi Nanga once again went to his farm and harvested a bunch of plantain. He peeled the plantains, cooked them with smoked deer meat, and put all the food in her *neshre.* She carried the *neshre* and was about to begin her journey when Cock asked her why she was leaving them so soon.

"I'm gone. I lay down in this house and I could not sleep. I could not lie down on my ribs. I could not sleep on my back. I could not lie on my stomach. I am leaving. I'm gone."

"On your way, if you see a pool dark as night, leave it alone. When you see the one that sparkles, stand on the bank and have a bath," Cock instructed.

Ajientoh ignored the dark pool and when she got to the pool that was as bright as a full moon she stopped, put her *neshre* down, and waded in. She ignored Cock's advice and lunged into the pool. She carried water in her palms and splashed her body. She would have liked to remain in the pool all day. Feeling somewhat refreshed, she got out and stood near the pool. While she waited for her skin to dry she saw a very old woman.

"Where are you from, my child?"

"Weeh! Where is this old woman from? Who are you? Are you supposed to know where I am coming from or where I am going? You, haven't I seen you before?"

"No, you're mistaken, my child."

The old woman walked away, leaving the girl standing by the pool. She soon forgot about the old woman as her eyes were fixed on the water. This pool looks so clean and bright, she whispered, I cannot go away without taking one last plunge. *Chuum!* in she jumped. To her surprise, masked spirits lifted her out of the water, caught her by the shoulders, and chased her out of the water. Ajientoh was terrified. She'd been touched by masked spirits, ancestors forbid! She bolted, abandoning her clothes and *neshre.* Manda thought she was hallucinating when she saw her sister run naked into the house.

"Weyeh! Is this how you went and were treated in that place? Is this how things were done to you? On the way I met pigs grunting everywhere asking me about my trip. Cats were meowing everywhere. Is that how you went? I saw that old woman, bent and brittle, sitting near the stream, asking me for food . . . was she waiting for me? I got to a man's house. He lives with a stupid cock. That man did everything with his buttocks. His buttocks were an entire universe unto itself. That butt cooked, cleaned, tapped palm wine, talked, talked, talked. Ants almost killed me at night when I tried to sleep. What a house! Is that how you were treated? Weeh! Weeh! I'd rather remain this way. I cannot do such a thing again."

"You kept complaining I had cheated you when I shared my beads. Why didn't you bring yours and have your revenge on me?"

"I cannot go to such a place again. I'd better stay here in my misery. Mamia-gheh. Please, sister-mine, give me some clothes."

"Yes, sister-mine, the one who grinds the corn gets a share of the mother's gruel. I cannot give you my clothes. You treated what I gave you the last time with contempt. Who goes on a journey and comes back empty-handed? In case you've forgotten, our mother always said that what you plant in the soil the soil gives you back in return."

When their father came home that evening, Ajientoh told him what had happened to her. He went into his house, found some rags and pieces of cloth, and handed them to his daughter. Ajientoh stitched them into a *njagasa*,[5] which she wore around her waist from that day forward.

This story is finished.

[5]Traditional Beba skirt, made out of numerous long strips—each about two inches wide—of different pieces of cloth, sewn together at the waistline only and worn by tying it around the waist like a wrappa (flowery cotton cloth, worn by wrapping around the waist).

The Girls Who Refused Suitors

For as long as I can remember, our people have always told *ble* recounting the lives of beautiful young women who foolishly believe that marriage is a contract between two people. They thumb their noses at the custom that valorizes marriage as the union of two families, a celebration of the joys that come with being part of a closely knit kinship. Our people measure wealth not by the property one owns but by the members of one's family. When girls are young they don't burden their minds with such details. No wonder the yarns people spin about them abound! Let us begin with a young woman who today owes her life to the kindness of a toad.

I

A woman and her husband had two children. One of them went to *alah akara*, the land of the whiteman. The sister he left behind missed him very much. She cried and pined for her brother's return. Baba, for that was her name, was a very beautiful girl. She was said to have the kind of beauty that made other women ill and made men mad. She grew into a buxom young woman and all the men wanted to marry her. They'd privately place bets and sometimes put on contests to see who in the end would be the victor. But Baba turned down the requests of all the eager suitors who came to ask for her hand. Men with cars, men with motorcycles, men with machines never seen in these parts; very handsome men came and knelt down before her, but Baba dismissed them all. One day, a dirty, ugly man came and offered his hand.

Baba looked at the man, contempt dancing on her brow, and said, "Many handsome men have come here for me and I turned them down. Why do you think I'd want to marry you? Go away. Leave our compound before I ask my father to throw you out."

The father, who was alarmed and unhappy at his daughter's behavior, looked at her and said, "My daughter, one who habitually peeps inside holes will one day be bitten by a snake the same way the chronic wandering dog will one day encounter a porcupine. I tell you this for the last time. Don't spit on other human beings. One of these days your ancestors will decide to put their hand in this and you will not like their verdict." He sighed and turned his back on his daughter.

The dirty, ugly man left quietly and transformed himself into a very handsome man. No man of his stature had ever been seen in the vicinity. He mounted his bike, rode into the village, and went back to woo the woman who had just rejected him. As soon as Baba caught sight of him, she was overjoyed.

"That's my husband. That's my husband. We are leaving immediately, right now," she told her mother.

"You can't marry this man," her mother complained. "You don't know this man. He does not know us. We do not know him. We do not know his family. How can you marry a total stranger? Why would you want to marry as if you were an orphan with no kinsfolk to stand by your side? You can't do this, my daughter."

"I can. I am," Baba retorted.

Baba's mother did all she could to dissuade her daughter. She fell down and cried—you'd think her daughter was dead. She rubbed wood ash on her body, a sign of mourning. Baba was as headstrong as a dog after a bone. Her mother put some corn-chaff in a calabash, handed the food to her daughter, and wished her a safe journey.

The bride and her husband mounted his bike and took off for his home. They rode on until they got to the banks of a river. Baba was so happy she didn't know how far behind they had left her village. All thoughts of her family seemed to rest in a distant past. The man stopped near the river, lifted his outer garment and asked her to give him the calabash of corn-chaff. He emptied the food into a deep pocket. He then lifted his shirt, scooped a handful of worms and gave his bride the worms to eat instead.

"Husband-mine, you're giving me worms to eat. Have I become an animal?"

"Eat!"

She reluctantly took the worms and ate them. He gave her a second handful. She made a great effort to eat them. He motioned and she got on the bike. They rode on until they arrived at his home. He led her into a house made up of seven rooms. This house looked so much like those houses she had heard described in *ble* when she was a little girl. She suddenly realized that the man she had married wasn't human. Confirming her fears, he kept her locked in the last room. He went outside and she heard his drumming. Sharp cries pierced the air, greeting the drum's message. Her husband's friends merrily hopped around the bush gathering firewood for the bonfire.

"Let's go away," Baba heard Magheb-the-Hawk whisper through a crack in the wall. "If you remain here, you shall be killed. Come, we must hurry," Hawk beckoned.

She declined his invitation, saying, "I will not leave my husband."

Detswegh-the-Toad hopped to her feet and beseeched her, "You'll die if you stay here."

Sensing real danger, Baba agreed to leave with Toad. He swallowed her deep into his stomach and stuck a hollow twig down his throat to help her breathe.

"What have you been feasting on, Toad? Look at your stomach. It's so swollen," the firewood gatherers queried Toad when they saw him passing through the forest.

Toad replied, "I've eaten my things. Are people supposed to ask others what they've eaten when they eat things that belong to them?" Toad scowled.

The ghosts ignored him. Toad hopped all the way to the river where Baba had eaten the worms. He heaved her up along with seven eggs. Toad broke six eggs in the river and the water parted into two. He gave her the seventh egg, recommending she break it when she sensed danger. Baba thanked Toad, descended the bank, and walked on the riverbed until she got to the other side. She was climbing up the riverbank when she heard them.

"There she is. There she is," the ghosts were shouting. They'd been searching everywhere after they made their fire and couldn't find her in the house. Ghosts have a strong sense of smell. She realized they must have smelled her the moment Toad heaved her up.

"How did she get there?" one of the ghosts asked when he saw her running across the riverbed. Led by her husband, they immediately rushed in, pursuing her as fast as they could. Baba scampered up the wall to safety on the riverbank. She watched the ghosts approach and broke the last egg Toad had given her. The parted waters came together, filling up the riverbed and sweeping the ghosts off their feet. Baba did not look back. She ran and ran until she arrived home. Her mother was surprised to see Baba, out of breath, run into the house and fall at her feet.

"Didn't I tell you not to marry that man? I ask you again, didn't I forbid you to marry that man?"

II

I was like Baba. I was also one of those girls who turned down the requests of all the suitors who came to ask for my hand. A boy who had only a head and no body left his village. Along the way, when he met people, he begged for and wore the body parts they offered him. First he got himself a new neck, then two arms, a torso, thighs, legs, and feet. He also borrowed a shirt, a pair of trousers, a pair of shoes, and a cap. All this I discovered only after I married him.

I was sitting in our compound when I saw this well-dressed young man coming up the hill. Something suddenly came over me. My heart beat with joy. I had never felt anything like that before I saw this dashing young man. I was drawn to him. I had to have him.

"We are going to die together," I screamed. "I've been turning down too many suitors. Today I've see the man I will marry," I said, shaking the boy's hand and welcoming him into our house.

"Father, I have turned away many men, but today I've seen the one I want."

Skeptical, my father asked, "Will you really marry him?"

"Yes. Tell him to bring my bridewealth and take me away."

My weary mother simply walked over to the man and said, "Come and finish the marriage negotiations and then you can take your wife with you."

Yes, this mother was tired of telling her daughter that the shaft of an arrow is sometimes feathered by one of the eagle's own plumes. The people were weary of this young woman's behavior and feared she could only come to harm. In fact, they learned the real story about what happened to her only after she returned to them, regained her voice, and told her story. She told of how she'd been saved from this unfortunate marriage.

The man who married her did fulfill all the demands made by Makuchi's family and took the happy bride away with him. The last they saw of them was the newlywed walking at her husband's side. After they'd covered a considerable distance, the village far behind them, Makuchi, to her great surprise, saw her husband give away his shoes. Before she could blink an eyelid he gave away the pair of trousers he was wearing, then his shirt, his cap, one arm, the other arm, one foot, the other foot, one thigh, the other thigh, his torso, his neck. All she had left for a husband was a head jumping *kro kro kro! Kakro! Kakro! Kakro!*

"A head? What happened to the man I married?"

She was alone and frightened, but she took heart and followed her husband to his village. Though she wanted to, she had come too far to go back home. Rats that live in a house do not feel smoke, she consoled herself. Many heads immediately encircled her in welcome. Some were hopping; others were jumping happily *kro kro kro! Kakro! Kakro! Kakro!* She watched them in awe. She was taken and locked up in a house. She could hear them arguing into the night about the day of the big event. They finally decided on the day of her death and maiden sacrifice. She was at a loss. What could she do to save herself as the day approached? Despair set in.

One night, she heard a voice in the darkness asking her why she had come here. It was an old raspy voice the girl did not recognize.

"Who are you?"

"I rule this village," the old woman's voice drifted toward her.

"I'm afraid. Are you here to help me?"

"What did the head do to convince and bring you here?"

The girl narrated her story: "I refused all the suitors who asked for my hand in marriage. One day, I saw this boy and told my father that he was the one I wanted to marry. I don't know why, but I was drawn to him. I wanted him at all costs. I did not know he was only a head. On the way here, he gave away his clothes and all the other parts of his body. I could not go back."

"Do you know something?"

"No."

"The day of your execution is already set. What will you do?"

"I don't know. My mother always says that prey attracts the fangs that are ready to devour it. I didn't listen to my mother and now I'm afraid I'm going to die," the girl replied.

"You should be afraid. Caterpillars only grow wings through death. I will play a trick," the old woman said and her voice faded into the darkness as stealthily as it had come. She went to see Magheb-the-Hawk and said, "You know there's a girl locked up in that house. I want you to go to that house on Nshialah. Make sure you get there in the early hours of the afternoon. At the time of the day when the sun has turned slightly away from our heads, you and your friends should come this way and save her from death." Hawk agreed to help, and the old woman gave him a bag of worms and a bag of termites.

On Nshialah, Hawk flew to the compound, accompanied by six of his friends. They perched in the branches of the huge cotton trees hugging the *nsaa*. The thick foliage hid them from view. The heads were all there, gathered in the yard, dancing around a girl standing in the middle of the circle. She was nervous. She was afraid the old woman would not fulfill her promise. She did lose hope, resigning herself to the sound of drums and certain death. The master drummer was relentless. He pounded away at the drum, making music and rousing the other heads to soporific exhaustion. They danced as if intoxicated by the lyrics. When their shadows were twice as long as their heads, they stopped and took a break to cool off. The gritty sound of a knife being meticulously sharpened was the only activity one could hear around the *nsaa*. But before the knife sharpener could slay the girl, Hawk swooped down, and off he flew with her in his beak. The heads heard the flop flop flop flopping sounds of huge wings, looked up, and watched helplessly as Hawk flew high, high, up into the sky. He was flanked by five others who took turns carrying the girl. They all soon disappeared from sight. The heads fell prostrate on the ground in lament. The old woman watched, not saying a word.

Hawk flew all the way to the girl's village. She screamed all the way with such joy that she lost her voice by the time they got her home. Hawk took her to her parents and told them all that had happened to her. It is said that Makuchi fell in love with Hawk and he fell in love with her. They got married with her parents' blessings and lived happily ever after.

III

The last story I'm about to tell you is the story of a young woman who refused suitors because she swore she'd never marry a poor man. "I want to marry a rich man. Why do men with no money come to ask for my hand? I must marry a man of wealth." She believed in the saying that a man who lives near a rich man is like a man who lives near orange trees whose fingers can reach only the thorns. She was determined to marry a wealthy man and so rejected all prospective suitors. She did not know she would one day get her wish. That day came sooner than she had expected. Her legend had traversed hills, valleys, and mountains and the raindrops carried it into the rivers where songs were made up about this young, wealth-seeking woman. It was then that three *mbwe* who heard and loved the song decided to win her hand. The fishes left the safety of the riverbed where they'd lived all their lives and took off for the girl's village. But first they begged for human trunks, feet, hands, eyes, and the clothes they wore. They even begged for a car and drove it to the girl's compound.

The minute she set her eyes on the car she was jubilant: "That is my husband. The man who is driving the car is my husband."

The three men were welcomed and treated as important guests. Tegheh-kwu! The marriage negotiations were completed that same day.

"Let's go," the girl said. "I cannot stay here one more day."

They left that very night. Dawn came and they were still on the road driving and driving. The journey seemed without end and the girl was getting impatient. The sun was almost overhead when her husband stopped at a compound. The girl jumped out of the car thinking they were home. To her surprise, her husband handed the car keys to the man of the compound.

"What will we do now that you've given away the car?" she asked.

"Don't you see that one tyre is flat? I want the tyre puncture repaired."

The girl took comfort in those words and they began their walk home. They had not descended a hill and crossed a river when he gave away his clothes.

"Why have you given away your clothes?"

"They are very dirty. I want them washed. I will come for them later," he replied.

Not long after that he gave away his hands. She asked him why he needed to do that, but her husband responded by giving away his feet and his torso. His brothers followed his example and gave away all their borrowed body parts. By the time they got to the bank of the river they had given away anything remotely human on their bodies and became three air-deprived fish. They hopped up and down on the riverbank, getting closer and closer to the water. At last she heard her husband's voice: "Go back to your parents. If you step into this water you will not be able to swim. Go back to your compound."

She did not respond. She burst into tears and sobbed like a hungry, sleepy child. Her husband repeated his command, but the girl only sobbed. The youngest of the *mbwe* began to sing:

Owerri go home ramara
We live in the deep ramara
She who cannot swim ramara
Will perish in the deep ramara

Owerri go home ramara
We live in the deep ramara
She who cannot swim ramara
Will perish in the sea ramara

"Go home," he repeated. "If you step into this water you will drown."

She did not move a step and he jumped into the water. The second brother asked her to go home. She did not move. He began to sing:

Owerri go home ramara
We live in the deep ramara
She who cannot swim ramara
Will perish in the deep ramara

Owerri go home ramara
We live in the deep ramara
She who cannot swim ramara
Will perish in the sea ramara

She stood her ground, tears rolling down her cheeks, and watched him jump into the water. He husband tried one last time, "Please go home. If you enter this water you won't be able to swim." She refused his offer and continued to cry. "Go home," he implored her again. "No," she said. He sang to her.

Owerri go home ramara
We live in the deep ramara
She who cannot swim ramara
Will perish in the deep ramara

Owerri go home ramara
We live in the deep ramara
She who cannot swim ramara
Will perish in the sea ramara

He finished this song and jumped into the water. She watched him glide gracefully; the water washing over his body. His scales shone, his eyes were bright, his tail wiggled, playful, as if saying one final good-bye, and then he disappeared from her sight. She stood there all alone on the shores and wept until she had no more tears. Only the knife knows what the cocoyam feels, she spoke softly, heaved a sigh, threw herself into the river, and drowned. The *mbwe* consumed her body.

So ends my story about three young love-seeking women.

Mbaka and the Magic Ring

A man and his wife lived happily with their son. The boy's father died while he was still a young boy. His mother died not long after. Mbaka was already of school-age when both his parents died. The aunt who was now raising him sent him to primary school.

At school, Mbaka loved one thing, playing football. His school team regularly participated in tournaments against other schools in the surrounding area. On one occasion, they had to play a football match in another village. The night before the match Mbaka had a dream and a voice spoke to him.

"You are going to play a tough match tomorrow. In the morning, go to the stream. You will see a piece of paper and a ring. Pick up the paper and read what's on it."

In the morning, Mbaka went to the stream. He saw a ring and a sheet of paper lying on a stone. He picked it up and it read: "You will have whatever you want with this ring."

Mbaka took the ring but did not go early to school as was his habit. Boys were sent to check on him but he told them to leave him alone. The teachers were furious at their star player's tantrum but there was nothing they could do. In the end, the team had to leave without him. After a long trek, the other players arrived at the field of play and were surprised to see Mbaka arrive at the same time. Though baffled, they were happy he was there. They changed into singlets and shorts and waited for the match to begin.

Spectators flanked the field and cheered the players on. They clapped, some jeered, and some whistled while taunting the opposing side. One of the young women standing by the sidelines keenly observed Mbaka and his skills. Whenever the ball went out of bounds, she was there to pick it up. She'd present the ball to Mbaka. At half-time, she invited Mbaka to their compound for refreshments. At the end of the match, she told Mbaka she wanted them to get married and took the young man to meet her parents.

"But I have just come here. How can you see me and propose marriage?" Mbaka asked, embarrassed by all her attention.

"I like you. I want to marry you."

"But you don't know me, and marriage is never done this way. How about courtship? How about getting to know your family, my family . . . ?"

"Marriage is for life. You'll get to know my family after we're married."

"But that's not the way a marriage is conducted . . ."

"Maybe not where you come from."

Mbaka addressed the girl's father. "Your daughter wants us to get married. What am I supposed to do?"

"You shall bring seven bags of *blah*."

Mbaka gave the girl's family the seven bags of cowries and took his wife home. With time, he grew to love her and his apprehensions slowly began to fade.

"What helped me get all the money I gave your father was this ring," he one day confided in his wife. "If I need anything and I hit this ring, my wish is automatically fulfilled."

On learning Mbaka's secret, his wife announced she wanted to pay her parents a visit. Mbaka offered to go with her, but she convinced him to accompany her on her next visit at the end of the competition season. Mbaka gave her presents for his in-laws and wished her a safe journey. Mbaka's bride returned home and disclosed her husband's secret to her father.

"Can you take it and bring it to me?"

"Yes, but how will I do that?"

"That's not a problem. I can give you some herbs that will put him to sleep," father reassured daughter.

She took the medicine and returned to her husband before nightfall. Husband and wife sat down to a lavish meal she had brought back with her. Before going to sleep, Mbaka took off the ring as was his habit and put it on top of the cane chair next to his bed. She waited for Mbaka to fall asleep and blew some of the medicine she had brought with her into her husband's nostrils. Mbaka fell into a deep, deep sleep. It was the kind of sleep the Beba say gets people lost in the land of the living-dead. Mbaka's wife took the ring and left for her parents' compound. Mbaka's faithful servants, a cat and a dog, saw their master's wife take the ring. The dog barked, the cat meowed, they barked and meowed around him, but could not wake him. Mbaka woke up the next day to the shock of what his wife had done. He immediately enlisted the help of the cat and the dog to rescue his ring.

"If we go and take it, Dog will want to keep it. He might see something on the way and bark and we'd lose it," Cat complained.

"If you take it and give it to me I will not bark," Dog assured Cat.

"I will give you whatever you want," Mbaka pleaded with them. "Please make sure you don't lose it."

Cat and Dog left for Mbaka's in-laws. They could hear drumming and drunken singing as they approached the compound. They got close to the houses and Cat asked Dog to wait for him in the bushes. Cat crept into the compound. His eyes surveyed the bloated feast the girl's father had thrown for his neighbors, friends, and relatives. The ring was prominently displayed on a chair next to him. Cat slithered quietly under chairs, slipped between legs, picked up the ring, and dashed out of the house. Mbaka's wife was the first to notice the ring missing. She suspected her husband's feline but she knew the cat was long gone.

While she pondered her next move, Cat made his way to meet up with Dog. As soon as Dog saw Cat, he started barking, asking for the ring. Cat refused to hand over the ring. Dog promised not to bark and Cat reluctantly gave him the ring. They took off for home. On their way, they arrived at a river and were about to cross it when they saw a fisherman hauling in a net full of fish. Dog spontaneously barked. The ring fell into the river and a fish immediately swallowed it. Cat could not contain his anger. He ignored Dog and begged the fisherman to catch the fish for him. The man threw in another net and caught the fish.

"Father, since this meat is so big, we'd like you to have it. But please gut it and give us the intestines," Cat and Dog begged him.

The kind fisherman disemboweled the fish and gave them the guts. Cat could see Dog eyeing the intestines. He insisted on carrying them himself. Dog reluctantly agreed.

When they got home, Cat narrated all that had happened and handed over the intestines to their master. Mbaka cleaned them out and found his ring. He threw a big feast in honor of his cat and dog. His wife eventually returned but Mbaka banished her from their home.

"Go back the way you came. It's true that a person's speed is best measured when they are pressed to go to the toilet. Go back! Tell your father I don't want my bridewealth back."

The story is finished.

The Dance in the Sky

This is a story about four daughters. One is an orphan. She lives with her three stepsisters. The sisters constantly snap at her. People say her sisters hate her because she is the prettiest of them all.

One day, their mother sends them to the forest to fetch firewood. The three sisters force their stepsister to do most of the wood-gathering. By midday it is so hot that they decide to go to the river for a swim. The orphan doesn't want to go but her sisters drag her to the river. The girls throw off their clothes and jump into the water. They water-drum and splash each other with handfuls of cold water. They scrub each other's backs and float on the water to rinse off. The orphan asks one of her stepsisters to scrub her back but the sister laughs at her and ignores her. Feeling rejected, she leans against an iroko tree and scrubs her back against its bark. Her back develops scales like those of a crocodile and wings grow out of her armpits. The girl falls down crying, rolling herself on the sand like a woman who has just lost her husband. Her sisters leave her there under the iroko tree and go home. When their father inquires about their sister's whereabouts, they lie. They claim she had gone to look for firewood in a different part of the forest. The man leaves in search of his beloved daughter and people say he never returned.

The girl cries all night, her wails echoing through the forest until an old woman hears her. She follows the sobs to the girl sitting under the tree. She takes the girl home and offers her her daughter as a playmate. She also offers her son in marriage. The girl is shocked by the offer and refuses to marry the old woman's son. "Why would any young man in his right senses want to marry me?" she wonders. The old woman cajoles her but she stands her ground. The old woman's daughter easily makes friends with the newcomer, but the brother despises her. He does not want to talk to her. He does not want to be seen near her. He calls her a monster as often as he bumps into her. The girl weeps bitterly at his insults.

"Before I join my ancestors, I want to see you married so I can go in peace," the old woman pleads with her son. The boy promises to get married but not to the monster with wings in her armpits and scales on her back.

"A wise man never urinates against the wind," she chides him. "Mark my words, your insensitivity will be your undoing."

One day, the orphan's friend announces that there will be a dance in the sky and she wants both of them to attend. This would be the orphan's first dance. The girl is hence excited about meeting other people. The two girls braid each other's hair. They bathe, dress in their best clothes, and leave for the event. They have to cross a river before arriving at the dance venue. When they reach the river, the orphan excuses herself, asking her friend to wait for her by the riverbank. She then hides behind a tree and metamorphoses into the beautiful girl she used to be, leaving the monster sitting under the tree. She rejoins her friend and they take off for the dance in the sky. All the young men admire the orphan. They all want to talk to her or dance with her. The old woman's son is one of those who think she is a queen sent to earth by the stars. The two girls enjoy the attention, dancing to the tune of *melo.*[1] They sing naughty songs to the moon and bawdy songs to the sun, leaving only when they are completely exhausted. On their way

[1]Beba traditional musical instrument; singular, *nelo;* plural, *melo.*

home, the orphan girl leaves her friend waiting by the riverbank and recovers her monstrous form. When they get home the old woman's daughter waits for her friend to go to sleep and whispers to her mother what she has seen that evening.

On the second night of the dance in the sky, the woman follows the girls and witnesses the girl's transformation process. During the festivities, the woman's son wants to dance with the new girl, but she continues to snub him. That night he does not sleep. He tosses and turns, tormented by thoughts of who this girl might be. How she resembles the monster!

On the third day of the dance in the sky, the old woman again follows the girls to the river. She hides behind a tree and waits for the orphan girl to enact her transformation ritual. When the girls leave for the sky, she burns the monster left behind sitting under the tree. She hurries back home, goes to bed, and pretends to be asleep. After the dance, the girl cannot find her monstrous form and knows she has been betrayed. Her friend apologizes to her and begs her to stay with them. Imagine what happens when the old woman's son sees the girl he has despised the following morning in their compound! He quickly proposes to her. She turns him down. But she adds, "If you bring me the tail of a living leopard, you can marry me."

"But that's impossible," he protests.

"Follow a river and you'll find the sea. And if you follow bees you cannot miss honey," she says and walks away.

The boy goes to his mother and asks for her help in solving the young woman's riddle. His mother rebuffs him. "The person suffering from diarrhoea is the one who goes to the bush," she reproaches him. The boy scowls. "How on my dead father's life am I going to procure the tail of a living leopard?" he screams at his mother. She purses her lips and turns her back to him. The boy walks around the village racking his brains, looking more miserable and haggard week after week. He approaches some of the elders, but the old men refuse to help him. One day he goes to the river to *leb ko'*[2] and while he is checking the fishing baskets he has an idea. He had once heard that leopards love honey. What better way to accomplish the task the girl has set for him? Isn't it said that a chick pries the hawk away from the top of the tree? His mood change doesn't go unnoticed by the villagers. He patiently waits for honey season, harvests a calabash, and carries it deep into the forest. He finds what he is looking for and waits near the grove for the leopardess to come out of her cave in search of food for her new cubs. When he hears her stir, he climbs up a tree and waits. The moment the leopardess appears under the tree, he drops some honey on her head, on her neck, on her jaw, and near her mouth. The leopardess tastes the honey, licks her whiskers, looks up into the tree, and asks the boy for more. He gives her half the contents of the calabash. She gulps the honey down and asks for more.

"I will give the rest to you on one condition."

"What do you want me to do for you?"

"I need the tail of a leopard to prove my love to the girl I want to marry."

"That's easy. I'll get you one, but you must promise to bring it back."

"I will bring it back to you," the young man promises.

The leopardess leads him into the cave. She gives some honey to her cubs. They eat it all and happily go to sleep. The young man cuts off the tail of one of the cubs and takes it to the girl. He tells her about the promise he has made. She gives him permission to take it back to the leopardess, who puts it back where it belongs.

A brawl erupts among the boys when they hear that the girl they all want is now going to marry the old woman's son. When they stop fighting, they confer, and decide to invite him on a

[2]Act of damming and constructing a wall in the river using stones and sticks to control the water flow and to hold in place fishing baskets; to lay fishing traps.

hunting expedition. They kill him in the forest and abandon his corpse there. When they return, they report that he has fallen off a cliff to his death. They tried but couldn't rescue him, they bemoan. The girl listens to their story and finally says: "I am going to throw a stone from the sky. Whoever catches it will be my future husband."

The young men sprint to the designated spot and jostle for position. The girl flies up into the sky and throws a big rock; some say the rock was heavier than *ngbalii.* The boys fight to catch it but the stone crushes them to death. The girl goes back into the forest, where she finds the boy's corpse and breathes life into the body.

It is said that from that day they both left the village and went to live in the sky.

This story is finished.

The Quest

"Are you listening?"

"Yes."

"Can an egg earn a young man a companion for life?"

"What?"

Many would laugh at this question the way you are laughing right now. They're right. So are you. An egg can do no such thing. But here is a story about a boy who grew up a long, long time ago without a father or a mother. The truth is, he did have parents. He also had a twin brother. It is said that before the twins were born their mother was one of those women disliked by the gods. None of the children she bore lived to see sunlight. There were whispers her womb was cursed. And then she bore twin boys. Chebe died at birth and their mother never recovered from his death. Funyi lived but was neglected by a father who spent the rest of his life mourning his wife. He had no ambition, acquired no land, and had no property to bequeath his son. For that reason Funyi said he had no father and no mother.

Funyi didn't dwell on his poverty. He was determined to be successful and, above all, not to die a bachelor. He learned to clear farms with other men and especially enjoyed hunting rat-moles. Digging for rat-moles was his specialty. He had the unique gift of spotting the right hole to dig when the beasts disappeared into an elaborate labyrinth of interconnected tunnels.

Funyi bragged that he was born with a knack for the geometry of a maze. You know what our people say about twins! This was certainly one of the gifts the gods bestowed on a twin. The Beba would say that the other twin's death must have awakened even more powers in him. Funyi never came home with an unsuccessful hunting story.

One day the boys went hunting and as usual they burned the grass and waited for the animals to run for what they thought would be safety. Of course, the animals simply ran into the blows of clubs and cutlasses. Funyi was not as lucky as the other boys, who successfully pursued and killed cutting-grass and rat-moles. His friends teased him, reminding him that missing a shot at a bird only gives the hunter tact. But Funyi scowled, and his anger got the best of him. He bragged that he was the best hunter of the group and refused to accept the wisdom that even expert hunters must time and again squat before they aim. He returned home hungry and despondent. He refused the food his father offered him and went to bed hungry.

The next morning, his stomach growled and growled and he couldn't stand the hunger any longer. He wandered about and came upon the old man who lived three compounds away. He stopped and asked the old man for food.

"Father," he said, "I am hungry."

"I have already eaten all the food I cooked," the man confessed. "What can I give you, my child? Go behind the house and pick an egg. Go find some firewood, roast it, eat it, and drink some water. You'll live, do you understand?"

"Yes father."

The boy thanked the old man and picked an egg from the pen. He bade the old man good-bye and walked away on what turned out to be a long journey. He thought staying would make him the village ninnyhammer, so he ran away from the other boys, choosing the ways of the landloper instead.

Funyi walked all night and all day. He crossed two rivers and came to a village where he met a man gathering and feeding hens—a whole lot of hens.

"Good morning, Father."

"Good morning. Where are you off to this morning?"

"I'm on a quest, Father."

"What would lead one so young on a quest?"

"I used to be an expert hunter. One day, I couldn't catch rat-moles anymore. That's what I want to find out. What have I done to my ancestors?"

"May the ancestors be with you."

"It's a bright morning. Why do you look so glum?"

"My hens have not laid eggs in months. They're restless because they have no eggs to incubate. Hear them go *kwak kwak kwak kwa kwa kwaakwakwakwa.* All that quacking and no eggs," the man complained.

Funyi put his hand into his raffia bag, pulled out the egg, and extended his hand to the man. "Here, take this egg and put it between your hens," the boy said. "They'll incubate the egg and you'll have some new chicks."

The man was very happy at the prospect of new chicks, but his hens went so wild with excitement over the egg, each wanting it for herself, that they fought over it and crushed the egg instead.

> Oh, look what has happened to my egg
> The egg the old man gave me
> The old man who staved off my hunger
> The terrible hunger that ate my insides
> The day I went hunting and returned without
> rat-moles

The man sympathized with Funyi and gave him an old cutlass. Funyi accepted the gift but decided to spend a few days in this village. He went on a stroll from compound to compound and came upon a builder toiling away at finishing a house. The man was hard at work making some mud bricks. He was using pieces of sticks to dig the red soil he mixed with water to make clay for the bricks.

"Is this how you build a house? Why are you using sticks instead of a hoe or a cutlass?" Funyi rudely interrupted the builder.

"I don't have any tools," the man replied.

"Here, take my cutlass. You will dig better with it."

The builder thanked him and started digging vigorously with the cutlass. In no time, he made mounds and mounds of mud, out of which he began to lay row after row of bricks. The builder was digging so energetically that the cutlass broke into two pieces. The man exclaimed and said, "Please forgive me. I'll find a smith to mend your cutlass." But Funyi wasn't listening. He immediately cried: "Look what you've done to my cutlass!"

> This is the cutlass the chicken farmer gave me
> The farmer whose hens broke my egg
> The egg that the old man gave me
> The old man who took pity on my hunger
> The hunger eating my insides because of a
>   fruitless hunting trip
> The hunting trip I made because my father
>   deserted me

The bricklayer listened to Funyi's story with much sympathy for the young man. He apologized and gave Funyi a long piece of bamboo. Funyi said good-bye to the builder and left the village. He slept two nights by a riverbank and woke up to see another village nearby. He was making his way into the village when he came across a man pruning plantain leaves using an elephant-grass stem. Funyi greeted the man with a lament: "In the days of our fathers and grandfathers, our people kept plantain stems clean by using a bamboo stick. They'd insert a knife on the tip of the bamboo and use it to pare the dead leaves. Why are you using a weak elephant-grass stem for such a job?"

"I don't have a palm bush," the man replied. "Where can I get a piece of bamboo when we don't have palm bushes in this village?"

Funyi offered him his piece of bamboo. The man quickly made a slit on one end of the bamboo stick. He inserted a knife through the slit and proceeded to pare off the brown-yellowed and sometimes torn plantain leaves. The more he worked, the better one could see the entire plantain farm. The men could feel the trees breathe. The cleaned stems shone bright gray and their young green leaves fluttered in the wind. The man was arduously working on a big leaf when he pulled too hard and the bamboo broke.

"Dead-Ancestors-of-Mine!" Funyi exclaimed. "What have you done to my piece of bamboo?"

> The bamboo the builder gave me
> The builder who broke my cutlass
> The cutlass the man gave me
> The man who broke my egg
> The egg the old man gave me
> The old man who calmed my hunger
> The hunger that burned in my entrails the day
> of the hunt
> The hunt I undertook because a father forsook
> his son

The man felt sorry for Funyi. He thanked him for coming to his aid and gave him a bunch of plantains. "I hope you can accept this gift from my farm," the man said. Funyi thanked the man and continued on his journey, carrying the bunch of plantains. He arrived at a stream where he met nursing mothers sitting near a *netreh*,[1] holding children's *shro*[2] in their hands. Funyi could tell they had no plantains or cocoyams to roast and eat with the palm oil. He offered them his bunch of plantains. They thanked him with *ashro mero.* Funyi put the *ashro* in his raffia bag and moved on.

On his way, his met *beh-nshi*[3] working on a woman's groundnut farm. They had just taken a break and were sitting down ready to eat some *achu* with *akiete* soup.

"Pity me!" Funyi exclaimed. "In the time of my mothers, before a woman invited *nshi* to her farm, she made sure she prepared good thick *achu* soup. A woman would not serve this watery thing you're about to eat. The women need to eat good food to work even harder on the farm. How can you be content with this *akiete?*"

"If we had palm oil, we would not be eating *akiete.* It's the rainy season and good palm oil is rare in these parts this time of the year," the women replied.

Funyi gave them his *ashro.* Without much ado, the women made thick *achu* soup with the palm oil and enjoyed a hearty meal. They thanked him with some bundles of *achu.* He wished the women a good day's work and went on his way. He happened to come upon a man feeding pigs with plantains. The man explained that the heavy rains had dealt a blow to their harvest and he could not afford to give his pigs a good meal of boiled *achu*-cocoyams. Funyi took all the *achu* bundles out of his bag and fed them to the pigs. The pigs grunted and fought for the bundles before they even touched the ground. They quickly

[1]Traditional palm oil mill.

[2]Calabashes used specifically to store palm oil; singular, *ashro;* plural, *shro; mero* meaning oil.

[3]People belonging to a social work group; *beh* meaning people; *nshi* meaning work group.

tore the leaves to pieces and fought over the *achu*, which they chomped down in no time. Funyi watched the pigs demolish the food and told the man his story. He told him how he had come to have the bundles of *achu.*

The *achu* that *bangie nshi* gave me
The women who used my *ashro mero* for their
akiete
The *ashro mero* the nursing mothers gave me
The nursing mothers who ate my plantains
The bunch of plantains the farmer gave me
The plantain farmer who broke my bamboo
The bamboo the builder gave me
The builder who broke my cutlass
The cutlass the man gave me
The man who broke my egg
The egg the old man gave me
The old man who calmed my hunger
The hunger that burned in my entrails the day
of the hunt
The hunt I undertook because my father had
forsaken me

The man caught a large pig, tied a rope around its neck, and gave the pig to the orphan. Funyi thanked the man and took the pig with him. The pig considerably slowed his pace and he decided to spend the night in the next village before continuing. Nothing prepared him for what he saw when he arrived at this village. The drums he could hear from afar told the story. The people were grieving, mourning the death of one of the daughters of the land. Funyi watched the villagers weep, catarrh running from their nostrils. When Funyi found out why the villagers were in such grief, he offered them the pig to be slaughtered in celebration of the young woman's life. The death celebration proceeded without a hitch. The people were grateful to Funyi for helping them mourn their daughter according to custom.

"What can we do to thank you?" they asked.

"You can give me the dead girl," Funyi replied.

They were taken aback by his request but because they had completed the rituals in honor of the dead, they gave him the corpse. She was now with the ancestors and her soul was at rest. The villagers continued to sing, dance, and invoke her spirit while Funyi washed the girl clean, perfumed her body, and took the corpse with him. At the village boundary, he invoked heavy rains and they were both drenched to the bone. He arrived at a palace shivering and cold. The king welcomed him and asked one of his wives, the most respected in the palace, to give Funyi shelter.

"Please, Mother, give me a bed for my child. It's been raining all day. We are both cold and need some rest," Funyi pleaded.

"Will your child not sit by the fire?"

"No, she's too tired. If you have a blanket, I will cover her with it."

The woman showed him to the bed of her own beloved daughter. Funyi put his bundle on it, covered it with a blanket, sat down on a stool near the fireside, and fell asleep. When the woman finished cooking the evening meal she woke Funyi up to eat. He ate alone and refused to wake up his child. He was then shown to a house where he spent the night. He woke very early the next morning and asked his hostess to wake up his child.

"You're asking me to wake up your child; have you greeted the king this morning?"

"The king is still sleeping. Must I wait for him?"

"There comes the king behind the house. Go and greet him," the woman interjected.

Funyi stepped outside and greeted the king. The king invited him into the palace. Funyi sat down and narrated his adventures to the court. He drank the palm wine the king's *ntsendia* kept pouring into his cup and profusely thanked the king for his hospitality. He told the king he wanted to leave before the sun reached the middle of the sky. The king sent word to his wife to wake up the child. The woman went to her house, tried three times, but failed to wake the child. A *ntsendia* was summoned, but he tried and failed as well. The king himself went into the room.

"She's dead," the king pronounced when he reemerged.

"What do you mean, dead? How did this happen?" Funyi screamed, stomping his feet like a spoiled child.

"We don't know."

"Mbeh, how did this happen? Are you talking about the child that the mourning villagers gave me?

The villagers who ate my pig
The pig the man gave me
The man whose animals ate my *achu*
The *achu* the *bengie nshi* gave me
The women who used my *mero* for their *akiete*
The *ashro mero* the nursing mothers gave me
The nursing mothers who ate my plantains
The bunch of plantains the farmer gave me
The plantain farmer who broke my bamboo
The bamboo the builder gave me
The builder who broke my cutlass
The cutlass the man gave me
The man who broke my egg
The egg the old man gave me
The old man who calmed my hunger
The hunger that burned in my entrails the
    day of the hunt
The hunt I undertook because a father
    forsook his son

Now you tell me I have lost a child in your home? Mbeh, my people say that two hands must wash each other. The one to whom you say hello with a smile in the morning might be the one who carries you across a flooded river in the evening."

The king had many daughters, but he was in a quandary. How was he to solve this dilemma? Which of his daughters would he give to this young man? He consulted with his wives, but their stony silence muted his request. The burden fell on the woman in whose house the dead girl had spent the night. But first the corpse had to be buried. After the burial the king decided to give the young traveler the woman's daughter.

Funyi thanked the king for giving him a life companion, but he did not leave. He stayed another week at the palace. Night after night, he told the girl his life's story. Each night, she listened as he narrated one story after another of the people he had encountered on his quest. Piecing together the events in his life, his adventures in the end endeared him to her. She agreed to be his companion only if he took her back to his village.

Before they left the palace, the king gave Funyi a special ancestral cup. He instructed them to use it to invoke the ancestors and pour libations whenever they were in need. Funyi returned home to the envy of his age-group. He poured libation in memory of his mother and his twin brother, Chebe. Only then did he live a life of prosperity with his wife and father.

The story of this young man's quest is finished.

Union Is Strength

There once lived an old man who had three sons. He named them Anyindep, Mbaka, and Jikwu after his father, his uncle, and his older brother. This father was unhappy for most of his life because his sons lived like cats and dogs. They were always at each others' throats. If their father asked them to do one thing or another, they would quarrel and quarrel and fight and nothing would get done. He would send them to the farm to clear the grass; one would come back with a swollen eye, another with a broken tooth, and the other with a wounded leg. He'd send them to the palm bush to tap palm wine. They'd fight over the jug of wine and come home with a broken calabash. The last time he sent them to the palm bush they came home empty-handed and drunk. Anyindep couldn't even remember where he left the tapping knife. Heavy rains are anathema to palm wine tapping. Tappers lucky enough to produce good wine from their *ntso* during the rainy season make huge profits. But the three sons never saw beyond their toes. The man could not help but curse his sons. Some said he was in such anguish that he wished the ancestral line would end with him.

It was at the height of the rainy season that the old man fell seriously ill. Half the crops were still in the fields and he was worried he might die without making peace with his sons. One day, he called the boys to his bedside and said, "My sons, I am a dying man. My heart smoulders inside of me for the three of you. It might turn to ashes right before your eyes. I know that when I die, you will kill one another. If I say, 'Bring me some water to drink,' you complain. 'Go plant some seeds in the farm,' you fight. 'Go tap some palm wine,' you tap your blood instead. It is a curse indeed to be here with you without my wife, your mother. I thank the gods every day that she did not live to see what irresponsible men you have become. She would have asked the ancestors to smite you herself. You are all like the man who fells forest trees and yet runs to the pathway and asks, 'Who's making all that commotion?' Yes, they say the mouth that ate the grain is the same one that asks, 'What shall I plant?' You, my sons, are young men who only want to swallow food that has been chewed for you. And even then you are incapable of swallowing. You're only good at hurting one another, forgetting that a stone that is thrown in the dark often hits a relative. I don't have the strength to call on the ancestors to rain their wrath on you, so I've decided to join your mother instead. But before I go, I'll give you one last task to perform for me. You, Anyindep, pick up that bundle of dry twigs lying on the floor by the hearth and break it," the father said in a feeble voice.

Anyindep picked up the bundle and fiddled with it. He held his hands out in front of him and tried to break the bundle. He bent double, sucked air into his lungs, puffed his cheeks, and made one last attempt.

"You fight with your brothers every single day," their father lamented. "I want you to display that strength right now."

Anyindep picked up the bundle again. He arched his back; his muscles contracted. Sweat dripped down his forehead. He threw the bundle down, wiped the sweat from his brow, and faced his father.

"Father, I have failed."

"What do you mean, you have failed," Mbaka scoffed.

"My brother, you shut up. You know what? The person who's carried on another's back does not appreciate how stiff the climb is."

"Mbaka, only yesterday you came home with a broken tooth. Show me how strong you are."

Mbaka, like his brother Anyindep, could not break the bundle of dry twigs. The old man then turned to Jikwu and pointed at the bundle of dry twigs. "It's your turn now," he said. Jikwu locked his ten fingers and cracked his knuckles. Satisfied, he picked up the bundle. He arched his back and strained his muscles; his biceps trembled and one of the twigs went crack. He groaned and tried again. Veins stood out on his forehead and neck. His jaws locked. Little red stars danced in front of his eyes. Finally, he screamed at his father: "Father, this bundle has defeated me."

"Look at you, whimpering like scavenger dogs. My son, a single stick smokes but does not burn. Have you ever heard that one hand cannot tie a bundle? That the shoulders cannot grow above the head? Pick up that bundle, put all your hands on it, and break the twigs together."

They did as they were told. They held both ends of the bundle together, untied the ropes holding the twigs together, and broke the bundle of twigs into two.

"My sons, our people say that life is like a river right after a heavy rainstorm. It prepares itself for the waters raging down gullies to flood its bed. When lips come together, the mouth whistles. When you act together you can always find a shoulder on which to rest your head. Union is strength. If you keep on fighting, you'll never become men. The more divided you are, the more you'll live miserable lives. I'm finished."

The father closed his eyes and was reunited with his wife. For once, the sons acted together and gave him a funeral befitting the father he had been to them all his life.

The story is finished.

Part 3

Penis, Testicles, and Vagina

"Nderr-the-Penis and Mberr-the-Testicles were very good friends. It was rumored that you could not see one without the other. They were like a palm branch and a cluster of palm nuts, for is it not known that the cluster rests on the branch?"

"You said it."

"People say they were like the head and the hand, neither sleeps without the other."

"Yes, like finger and nail."

"On this day, our two friends go fishing at nki Mbu. You know nki Mbu; the river has a reputation for the big *mbwe tseb* nesting in its bowels. The Beba say a man can chew his fingers off eating this mudfish when cooked by a real Beba woman . . ."

"Yes, a Beba woman who can't cook this fish isn't a woman . . ."

"So, our two friends go fishing and catch a lot of *mbwe*. It so happens that on their way home they meet Nekwerr-the-Vagina. No one knows where she's coming from. She won't say either.

"'Has the evening touched your faces?' she greets them.

"'And yours too?' they greet back.

"'Where are you coming from?'

"'We went fishing at nki Mbu.'

"Vagina begs for some of the succulent fish whose flesh is as white as a Calabar yam. The friends aren't too happy about parting with some of their *mbwe tseb*. After some hesitation, Penis decides to give Vagina some of his catch. He tells himself,

'You cross a river easily in the morning but on your return in the evening you might find the river flooded and the man you greeted with a sweet tongue in the morning will carry you across.'

"Testicles, however, refuses to give Vagina any of his fish. He complains that the fishing expedition was a disaster. The mudfish would not leave the comfort of their warm muck, he fibs. Testicles reasons that one does not feed a fowl on the day one takes it to the market. After all, people say that a person who loves to eat fish should learn to be a fisherman; one who eats a lot of meat should learn to be a hunter. 'We didn't catch much,' he lies again to Vagina. Vagina thanks Penis. She tells Penis she'll smoke the fish and then invite him to a meal.

"The rainy season that year is uneventful but the dry season comes hot on its heels. The heat that year is so harsh the sun burns all the grass on the hills. Luckily, the planting season is still a few moons away. It is during that short period of rest preceding the clearing of the land and the planting of crops that Penis and Testicles leave for Bombe to visit some relatives. They know if they miss this opportunity, they'll have to wait for the rest period after the next harvest season. Their trip goes well. They find their relatives in good health and are thankful. They begin their return journey on a Nshialah. It is very hot and villages where they can stop to rest are few and far between. But fortune often smiles on the man who sows good seeds in his farm.

"It so happens that the two friends meet Vagina, who had gone to the stream to carry some water. When Vagina sees them huffing and puffing under the sun, she reminds herself that when a river travels alone it often meanders and she offers Penis shelter from the flaming sun. Penis is overwhelmed with so refreshing and comfortable a refuge. Testicles begs and cries and pleads with Vagina for a little relief."

"And what does she say?"

"Vagina gives him a few drops of her water. He gobbles them up and pleads for more. She tells him to content himself with what she's offered or she'll cut him off. She does, however, remind him of the saying that dirty water also puts out a fire. 'Be grateful that I'm going to stay friends with your friend,' she teases him."

"Yes, she is right. It's what a man puts in the earth that the earth gives him back in return, isn't it?"

"We now know that from that day, every time Penis and Vagina rendezvous, or accidentally meet, and Testicles by chance tastes of her generosity, he clings desperately to her, promising never to be selfish again."

This story is finished.

When You Eat Today, Remember There Is Tomorrow

There was once a small village. A man lived in this village of a few hundred people. His name was Chebe. Hmm, Chebe was known throughout the village for his long throat, his greed. Every edible thing that crossed his path, that he laid his hands on, wound its way down his throat. A piece of bone once planted itself in that throat and were it not for Agheyih, the healer, and his timely intervention, Chebe would have been forgotten.

Do you remember the proverb that mocks those individuals who have scabies but no nails to scratch them? Well, Chebe was one such fool. He had a kind wife, Male. She knew her husband loved food and she always cooked huge quantities for him. You'd think she cooked every day for ten children. One day, she cooked some *meker dze* for her husband before leaving for the farm. When Chebe ate the entire pot of peas his wife had prepared for him, he was still as hungry as that Leopard who was caught in a hunter's trap for three long days until Monkey came along to save his life . . . But that's another story. Chebe took some more of the *meker dze* from his wife's *detene*,[1] filled a pot, and put it on the fire to cook. When he was certain that the pot of *meker dze* was well cooked, he drained the water

[1]A rectangular storing place that hangs from the ceiling directly above the fireplace.

and poured the beans into a small *aki*, the type of mortar women use to blend spices. He then added salt, *feleb*,[2] and hot pepper to taste. He put so much palm oil in the beans that you'd think it was meant for a new bride or a birth celebration. Then Chebe did the unthinkable. Ancestors forfend! He shut the door. Dead-Father-of-Mine! He shut the door, in broad daylight. He pulled a chair, sat near the mortar, and started eating. He ate, and ate, and ate. He watched his stomach bulging out, gaining volume progressively, until he felt pains in his bowels. But he would not stop. Chebe would not keep some of the food for anyone else, not for visitors, not even for his wife. As you can imagine, he did not share with his ancestors either. Chebe must have thought his stomach was as elastic as the Mother Earth's. You know what the proverb says; the earth's stomach is never satiated with corpses. We are only human and stomachs do have their own limitations. But what human would shut the world out while he ate? Chebe kept on eating, not noticing the oncoming disaster, for *pwaaaaaaaaahhh!* his stomach exploded. All the food he had been eating slowly meandered its way back into the *aki*.

When Male returned from the farm, she was confronted with the gruesome spectacle. Truly it's only when the wind blows that the fowl's anus is exposed. Male was dumbfounded by her husband's behavior. She wept, she cried, she sang, calling for her neighbors, calling on her ancestors:

My husband is a glutton oh yang
My husband is a glutton oh yang
If I am the one, I eat and give you some, oh yang
If you are the one, you eat and give me nothing
oh yang ke ke le kwo oh yang
ke ke le kwo oh yang

[2]Known as traditional onion, it is obtained from the bark of a tree; like cinnamon.

ndeb ghe eh ndzi nkwu oh yang
ndeb ghe eh ndzi nkwu oh yang
a bwo me ma dzi nfia gho o yang
a bwo gho gho dzi nyub a ghe
yang ke ke le kwo oh yang
ke ke le kwo oh yang

My husband eats and dies, oh yang
My husband eats and dies, oh yang
When I eat, I share with you, oh yang
When you eat, you do not share with me, oh yang
ke ke le kwo oh yang
ke ke le kwo yang

They say the stomach of a stranger is like a small horn: it cannot empty your granary. Male had lived her life in the spirit of this proverb. How could she fathom that such a deed would occur in her own home? How does a woman let go of her grief when she has to tell her people that her husband, the man who lay down by her side every night, died because of *meker dze;* that he died because of gluttony; that he died because of his selfishness? I would not want to be in her shoes.

This story is finished.

The Greedy Mother

A mother once went to a feast organized by one of her friends; a feast in honor of her son's naming ceremony. This mother had had her own baby a few months earlier. The baby was now learning how to creep. She didn't want to leave her baby behind, so she strapped him on her back with a colorful wrappa, placed the basket of food she was taking to her friend on her head, and the two were off to the ceremony. When she got there, she warmly greeted friends and relatives, untied the baby from her back, and sat down with a group of women. Food was served in large quantities to all who had come to welcome the newborn. Our visiting mother drank and drank but not a drop of palm wine did she give her child, despite the fact that the child was wide awake watching morsels of food disappear down her throat. Not once did she think of dipping her finger into the soup and putting the finger into her child's mouth. Not once did she think of dipping her finger into her cup and putting a drop on her child's tongue. The feasting came to an end and it was time to go home. The woman carried her baby on her back, put her now empty basket on her head, said her good-byes, and left for her home. Not long afterward, they arrived at a big crossroads. The woman thought she heard her child speak.

"Please, Mother, put me down," the voice entreated a second time.

The woman was terrified and did not know what to do. This child is barely creeping, not to mention walking—how can he talk? She loosened the loincloth and put the child down. She blinked and there, right in front of her, was a grown man. The mother was petrified but she could not run away.

"Follow me," the man told his mother.

He took one of the roads and his mother followed fearfully. The road came to an abrupt end in a large compound. The woman saw children run up to her child shouting, "Welcome Father. Welcome Father." Their mother greeted her child as her husband. The man quietly returned their greetings and went to work, slaughtering goats and pigs. He handed the meats to his wife, asking her to make food for their visitor. The man's daughter pounded some *achu* while his wife used the goat meat to make thick spicy *achu* soup. They invited the visitor to eat with them. The child's mother ate till she could eat no more. At the end of the meal, he took baskets from the *nekaa*[1] and packed them full of things for his mother. He also gave her some goats and told her it was time for them to leave.

The woman was puzzled: "This child I carry on my back has a compound, with a wife who calls him husband and children who call him father?"

As if he heard her, the man warned his mother, "Do not tell anyone what you've seen here today. However, you are always welcome back here," he added.

When they got to the big crossroads, the man became a baby again and asked his mother to carry him. She carried the child on her back for the rest of the journey. Her arrival brought out curious relatives and friends. They wanted to know what or who was the source of all the things she brought back with her.

[1]The ceiling; specifically, the space between the ceiling and the roof, where things are kept out of sight and food such as dried groundnuts, corn, beans, and so on are stored.

She smiled and said, "An elder does not break wind in public." But they weren't appeased. They knew she couldn't have brought those things from the naming ceremony. The most she could have brought back from such a ceremony would be a bottle of beer or a piece of meat carefully wrapped in a plantain leaf, not a herd of animals and baskets full of things. When a man brings home a piece of kola nut he tells his people the name of the person who gave it to him, one of the woman's relatives pointedly noted. A river that travels alone often meanders, another chimed in. But the mother maintained an eerie silence. They pestered her like a red jigger but all they got from her were presents. The woman gave away all the gifts she had brought with her to the men, the women, and the children in the entire compound. That way, she has protected her secret unto this day.

This story is finished.

The Ring and the String of Beads

It was toward the end of the dry season, the period when women gathered grass, burned their farms, tilled the land, and planted seeds. One woman wanted to sow pumpkin seeds but she didn't have enough *nkra.* These wooden or earthenware rings were placed around young plants to protect them from insects in their early growth stage.[1] Ngonda, for that's her name, went to her friend, Bishi, and begged for a *nkra.* Her friend and neighbor gave her the *nkra,* which she happily took to her farm and used to protect her pumpkin seed. The seed sprouted and grew into a very healthy plant. The leaves of this particular plant were as large as cocoyam leaves, for they flapped loudly at the softest rustle of the wind. As one would expect, its beautiful, fragrant yellow flowers and huge buds produced large pumpkin pods.

Bishi eyed her friend's plant with anger and envy. The more people talked about Ngonda's pumpkin plant, the more Bishi was green-eyed. And so, one bright sunny morning, she went

[1] *Nkra* are round and made with the bark of palm branches or the recycled necks of discarded or broken earthenware pots. When modern sieves are bad, the netting at the bottom of the sieve is removed and the round wooden frame can serve as a *nkra. Nkra* are also used as support for the bottom of a calabash (such a gourd would hold palm wine or palm oil), as support for an earthenware pot hot off the fire, or as support for an earthenware pot holding water or palm wine that is served to a seated group of people.

to Ngonda's house and knocked on the door. Ngonda opened the door and was surprised to see her friend.

"Has someone died?"

"No."

"What then? Is your daughter sick?"

"No. I just want my *nkra* back."

"Mumia gheh! Sister-of-Mine! I can't give you the *nkra*. Please be patient. Once the pumpkins have matured, I'll pick them and give you your *nkra*."

"I want my *nkra* the way it was when I gave it to you," Bishi replied and turned her lips to the sky.

"But you are not planting any pumpkin seeds yourself. Please give me one month, my sister . . . just one month," Ngonda beseeched Bishi.

"Don't waste your time begging. That won't help."

"We will share the vegetables, if that's what you want," Ngonda supplicated.

"Give me back my *nkra*! I don't want your stupid pumpkins," Bishi screamed, plugging her ears with her thumbs.

Ngonda could not get hold of the *nkra* without destroying her pumpkin plant; the stem had far outgrown the protective ring. Faced with Bishi's determination, she had to do the unthinkable. She went to her farm with tears in her heart and a heavy hand; some remarked her hand must have weighed more than a *ngwalii* stone. Ngonda raised her cutlass and felled the plant. She sobbed as she watched the once robust plant wither in the sun. Bishi collected her *nkra* and her heart sang all the way home.

Days passed, months passed, rainy seasons paved the way for dry seasons; years crawled by as people worked on their farms, rested after each harvest, and women birthed and raised children. The ancestors finally blessed Bishi, this woman who had had three daughters, with a son. Who can measure such joy? Bishi threw a feast for her son. Only one thing dampened her spirits. She did not own any of the special strings the Beba wear around a newborn's neck; not those made of beads known as *nkre jigida* or *findi ntsa*, not even the modern red bangles known as *ndegh waba*. These strings and bangles hold and firm up the child's neck; they strengthen the neck bones and posture; they have the power of protecting the child from illness and evil spirits. Bishi fretted all week and the answer to her problem finally dawned on her. How could she have forgotten?

Ngonda was the best *nkre*[1] weaver in the village, a task she performed from time to time, usually weaving during the period of rest. The finest *nkre* had to be woven thin and the texture had to be soft and firm. Bishi ran to Ngonda's house to elicit her help. She knocked on her friend's door and asked her for a string of beads.

"Why don't you buy one of those modern red bangles, not the white ones, mind you. You know the white ones bring bad luck," Ngonda suggested. "Those things are easy to maintain and adjust as the child grows older."

"I'd rather you weave one for my son using the *ndia tou* threads from our forest."

"I might have one here," Ngonda replied. She offered Bishi the *nkre*, which her friend proudly put around her son's neck. She was now secure in her son's protection and healthy development.

Bishi's son indeed grew into a plump, lively boy. His cheeks were said to shine like the egg of a python, words that warmed his mother's heart. She offered daily libations to the ancestors, thanking them for this son who would take care of her after her daughters had married into other families. One early morning, Bishi was busy cooking the morning meal in preparation for a long day of farmwork when she heard a quiet knock on her door. She stepped over a log burning in the fireplace, pushed

[1]Rope; in this case, a specially woven rope worn around the neck as is or beautified with beads.

open the door, and peered at a silhouette hugging the open door, hidden behind the veil of smoke.

"Who is it?" she asked, wiping the smoke sting from her eyes. She stood erect, squinted at the door and stared into Ngonda's eyes. Her heart missed a beat. They say if you see a snake silent by the wayside you know it has swallowed its prey. Ngonda's eyes bored holes through her head. Bishi feigned a smile.

"I have come for my *nkre jigida.*"

"Good morning, my sister," Bishi replied, as if she had not heard Ngonda.

"Good morning."

"What brings you here so early in the morning? I was just getting ready to leave for my farm."

"You heard what I said. I've come for my *nkre jigida.*"

"Eh! You want your string back? But how can I give it to you without harming my son?"

"A snuff-box has no right to sneeze. Only you have the answer to your question."

Bishi cried and sniffed and cried.

"*Tsa-tsa.* Please. Ngonda, he is a child. He is a human being. He is the only son I have. Please, let me cut the string. You can weave it back together . . ."

"What? No, you can't do that. I want it whole, the way it was when I gave it to you."

"Please, Ngonda. I will buy you another one . . ."

"I don't want another one."

"What then can I give you as adequate compensation?"

"My friend, you should have known not to cut a tree that is covered with ants. That's why our people say that if you sleep with fowls you will smell of fowl droppings."

"Ngonda, tsa tsa, he is a child," Bishi moaned.

Ha ha ha ha ha, Ngonda guffawed and said, "Do you remember my pumpkin? It's true that if you keep scratching the anus you'll touch excrement. Hurry up! The sun is already up and the weeds are eating up my groundnuts."

Bishi slew her son and gave Ngonda the *nkre jigida.*

This story is finished.

The Huntress

Once, a woman lived with her three children, two girls and a boy. Every evening she'd feed them, put them to sleep, then transform herself into one animal or another and go hunting. One day, as she was about leave for the hunt, she asked her children, "If you don't see me today what will you do?"

"Today, if you do not return, we will mourn you," the children replied.

The woman gave her children a large *akekeh lah*[1] and went hunting *beko*. She deliberately stayed too long in the forest. The children waited and waited for their mother's return. They soon gave up hope. The oldest child took the *akekeh lah* she had given them and wept:

anga nele o ki ya eh
anga nele o ki ya eh
anga nele o kiya oh
anga nele o kiya oh
mangie lio ma jwe mo yi nzwete le e?
mangie lio ma jwe mo yi nzwete le e?
mako kwan ma ko sito o
mako kwan ma ko sito o
ma ga yer beko kwan ya se?

[1]When a calabash or gourd is halved, each round half is a traditional bowl known as *akekeh lah*—bowl of the land, i.e., not imported, modern, or Western.

anga nele o ki ya eh
anga nele o ki ya eh
anga nele o kiya oh
anga nele o kiya oh
Has a woman ever delivered a child of hers and killed it?
Has a woman ever delivered a child of hers and killed it?
mako kwan ma ko sito o
mako kwan ma ko sito o
What will I do hyraxes kwan ya se?

She filled the bowl with tears, emptied it, and gave the bowl to her sister. The sister wept, holding the bowl below her chin. She cried, filling the bowl with tears until she had no more tears to shed. She threw away her tears and handed the bowl to her brother. Rather than follow his sister's example, the boy rebuked his mother: "If our mother has transformed herself and gone to hunt rock-hyraxes, let them kill her. If Mother-Mine has transformed herself and gone to hunt rock-hyraxes, let *ndafo* carry her.[2] If our mother has transformed herself and gone to trap *nenaa*, let those civet cats tear her to pieces. Mourn your mother. I will not weep for her."

The mother finally returned after several days in the forest. She asked her children if they had mourned her. "Yes, Mother, we did," the girls answered in unison, concealing the truth about their brother's behavior.

"If that's true, you should mourn now so I can see for myself," she insisted, picking up the bowl and handing it to her oldest daughter. The child wept and gave the bowl to her sister, who did the same. The boy cursed his mother instead: "If

[2]When a Beba has a dream and sees a spirit-ghost carrying this or that person it implies that the person is either dead or about to die. The spirit-ghost is simply taking the person into the world of beyond.

our mother went to hunt rock-hyraxes, they should kill her, tigers should tear her to pieces, civet cats should carry her."

"What kind of a child are you?" the mother asked, beating her son. "You don't want to do what I ask of you?"

The boy sulked, left the house, and started crying. The mother went after him.

anga nele o ki ya eh
anga nele o ki ya eh
anga nele o kiya oh
anga nele o kiya oh
mangie lio ma jwe mo yi nzwete le e?
Has a woman ever delivered a child of hers and
killed it?
mangie lio ma jwe mo yi nzwete le e?
Has a woman ever delivered a child of hers and
killed it?
mako kwan ma ko sito o
mako kwan ma ko sito o
ma ga yer beko kwan ya se
What will I do hyraxes kwan ya se?

The woman followed the direction of her son's voice, calling his name. The boy ascended a hill, descended another, and got to a village farm, where a man called Nanga Batebe captured and killed the child. When the boy's mother got to the top of the hill, she again called out to her son. This time she no longer heard his voice. "Why do I always taunt my children with death?" she scolded herself as she descended the hill. She finally came upon Nanga Batebe's compound.

"Father, as you were sitting here, did you see a child come this way? A little boy."

"No," Nanga Batebe replied. "I heard some children talking in the palm bush, some were running down the stream. I don't know whether your child is among them. Please come in and eat a piece of plantain."

The woman entered the house, sat down, and Nanga Batebe served her some plantain and meat. She thanked him, removed a small piece of plantain, and tossed it on the ground in offering to the ancestors before putting a piece of meat into her mouth. But something rather strange happened. Each time the woman put a piece of meat in her mouth she heard a bird perched somewhere on the roof say, "You're eating the flesh of your child's body." She'd throw the piece of meat down and remove a piece of plantain. Again, the bird would sing-song as her hand made its way to her mouth, "You are eating plantains of your child's body," and she'd hastily throw the piece of plantain back into the dish. The bird's voice seemed to be coming from different directions. Her eyes searched the trees in the *nsaa*. She peered at the branches but she couldn't see the bird. "Where is this bird hiding?" she whispered. She stood up. Her gaze roamed the canopy of leaves, but her tormentor remained hidden from sight. That voice seemed to be rising from within the trunks of trees in the yard. It almost seemed to be rising from within her. She thought she was daydreaming, but Nanga Batebe's soothing voice calmed her worries.

"Do not worry about our birds," he told her. "You are a hunter. You know they're harmless. If you care about what they say, you won't eat a thing in this village. Our birds have always been like that, incommodious."

The woman hesitated, sat down, and removed a piece of meat. When she was about to sink her teeth into it, the bird sang, "You are eating the meat of your child's body."

"What birds can these be? Birds that wait for the moment when I want to eat a piece of meat to say such a thing?"

She threw down the piece of meat and jumped up. As she hurried out of the house, her host, with one blow, chopped off her head. The head fell outside into the *nsaa* and the rest of her body fell inside the house.

"My meat has come again. So, the other one was her child?"

Nanga Batebe groaned as he watched the bird swoop down and fly away with the huntress's head. The bird flew over hills and trees, not stopping to draw breath. He took the head to his sisters and disappeared into the night. The girls kept watch over their mother's head until they fell asleep. Only then did the head transform into the mother who had gone after her son. It is said that from that night she never went hunting again.

This story is finished.

King-of-Scabies

Our people say a hyena does not eat its young, irrespective of hunger or greed, but this story is about a people who, like lions, feed on their kind. A long time ago, in a village about eight days' trek from here, there lived a people who ate human flesh. This village looked like any other with its hills, valleys, rivers, thatched roofs, and compounds. The one thing out of the ordinary was a big house at the center of the village. It is said that victims who had been hunted and captured were killed and consumed in that house. The men took turns to go in search of their prey. They'd carry the victim in their *bendjob*[1] all the way back to the house at the center of the village. The man would then go to the palace and inform the king of his successful hunt. The king would immediately beat the drum *dum dum dum dum*, calling all the men, *gwudum gwudum gwudum gwudum* to congregate for the feast. Dead-Father-of-Mine! I tell you, if the king had to play the drum himself then this village surely must have been cursed.

One day, one of these cannibals went to a village far, far away and abducted a young girl. She was an only daughter. The child had been left at home while her parents went to the farm. The man put the little girl in his *bendjob* and left for his village. That evening, the child's parents came back from the farm and looked for their daughter everywhere in the village

[1]Literally, that which is carried on the back; a bag that is carried on the back; a backpack.

and the surrounding communities. They searched every compound, they searched the hills, they searched the forests, but their efforts yielded nothing. There was no sign of the girl anywhere. As the days passed and the season began to fade, the village slowly lost any hope of finding the girl. They concluded that she might have been attacked by a wild animal and was probably dead. They poured libations and proceeded with the death celebrations.

But something strange happened a few days after these celebrations. As you know, there is nothing as hollow as the silence of death that engulfs the bereaved when the community leaves right after the final death rituals have been performed. Some neighbors of the grieving mother decided to ask her to go farming with them. They were going to make beds for planting sweet yams and *achu*-cocoyams. "You need to get out of the house," the woman's neighbors insisted. "Leaving the house will ease your pain," they cajoled. The grieving mother agreed and they all left for the farm far, far away from the village. One good thing, the farm was located close to the main path used by the many villagers who farmed in that area. The grieving mother was certain to see many of the people who had condoled with her not so long ago.

It so happened that the man who had stolen the child used that same path while they were working. He greeted the women, "My mothers, I commend your work."

"Eeh loo," they greeted in unison.

"I am very hungry. Would you please give me some food? I will eat it, give some to my bag, and it will sing for you," the man said.

The woman who had lost her child hurried to a bed below the farm and harvested some cocoyams. She carried the cocoyams to one of the huge rectangular beds that the women had made that morning by piling large amounts of grass and twigs into big heaps and covering them with mounds of soil. Each bed had two open ends where they lit a fire to slowly burn the grass as they worked all day long. The woman moved closer to the beds, carefully examined the openings for the best spot to roast the cocoyams. She picked up a piece of stick, pushed it into the fire, moving the stick from right to left, widening the mouth of the bed that was already filling up with hot ash. She absent-mindedly thought about how the fire would continue to burn for days. For days they would continue to use these smouldering beds as ovens to roast either yams, cocoyams, sweet potatoes, plantains, cassava, or plums while they worked on other parts of the farm. The woman sighed and hurriedly widened the hole. She tossed the cocoyams into the hot ashes. The skins rustled. They could all hear the cocoyam skins go *twa, twa, twa, twa, twa, twa.* The woman used the piece of stick in her hand to turn the cocoyams over from side to side, listening attentively to the soft crackling sounds. When the sounds went dead, she removed the cocoyams from the fire and took them to the hungry traveler. The man peeled and ate them, opened the mouth of his *bendjob*, and gave the peelings to the girl.

"Eat and sing for these women," he ordered.

The little girl took the peelings, put them together at one corner of the bag, and sang her village song, in their language. She sang in a soft, sad voice.

tanda meyase djo
misi yie
u fiake mi boro wato
wandele wa, wandele selenge
wandele senge senge[2]

The woman listened very carefully and thought she recognized her daughter's voice.

[2]This is not Beba. My mother often told this story. She taught us this song but said she did not know what language this is.

"Your bag has such a nice sweet voice and sings a marvelous song. Can you ask it to sing again?" the woman requested.

The man ordered the little girl to sing.

tanda meyase djo
misi yie
u fiake mi boro wato
wandele wa, wandele selenge
wandele senge senge

"Please give me some water to drink," the man said, scratching his throat.

The cocoyams had not been well cooked and the man had eaten them so quickly he was now feeling an irritating itch on his palate and in his throat.

"Ta,[8] I am sorry. I do not have any water. Our water is already finished. I beg you, take this calabash. That is the spring a few steps away, just ahead, in front of us. Just three furrows across," she told the man, pointing at a spring. "Go over there and quench your thirst and please bring some water for us."

The man saw the spring and took the calabash. As he walked and got closer to the spring, the woman made the spring move further away. The more he hurried his steps, the more the spring receded from view. Soon, he disappeared from sight. The woman hurriedly opened the *bendjob*, removed her daughter, and hid the child behind a thick shrub. She then created a swarm of bees, filled the bag with them, and closed the mouth of the bag. She made the spring return to its original location. The man drank his fill and, turning around, saw the women three furrows away from him. He did not know that he had walked across the plain and back. He brought some water to the woman, who took the calabash, thanked him, and drank some of it. He said good-bye to the women, got hold of

[8]Respectful form of address, meaning Father.

the *bendjob*, but, as he was about to carry it, remarked it was very heavy.

"Idiot, maggots will eat your intestines! You will die of dysentery," he said. "You have eaten so much of these women's food that you are now as heavy as *ngwalii*," the man cursed. "*Ngo'o*[4] will be put on your chest tomorrow."

The answer to his curse was a prolonged hum of bees.

"Have you eaten so much that all you can do is hum like bees?" the man asked furiously, lifting the *bendjob* with all his strength.

He carried the *bendjob* over both shoulders, letting it drop in such a way as to fit flat on his back, the two ropes on both sides of the bag running securely from his shoulders down his armpits. This stop was the first of many he made during his long journey home. When he had walked a considerable distance and felt tired and hungry, he stopped and asked the women in their farms to give him some food and water. And at each stop, he asked the child in his *bendjob* to sing. The bag would hum its song. Though irritated by this erratic behavior, the man endured the humming *bendjob* until he got to the house of festivity. He went straight to the king and broke the good news. The king mounted the ceremonial drum, beating it with all his might, calling for an assembly of all the men of the village. Believe me, I am certain this village was cursed. Why would a king not let his pages, why would he not let his *ntsendia*,

[4]Literally: an extremely heavy stone; also used to refer to the *ngwalii* stone—basalt—used in making huge sculptural pieces for the fon's palace. Figuratively: when the Beba say, "The *kpwefo* has placed *ngo'o* on someone's chest," it means the sanction of death—the ultimate punishment for unpardonable crimes—has been decreed for that person and is carried out by the *kpwefo*. In modern-day Beba, the sanction of death is sometimes replaced with banishment from land, the culprit stripped of all titles and benefits of his clan. The compound and property of the exiled person revert to the fon (see *kpwefo*, page 166, note 1).

do their jobs? A king cannot mount a drum, not when he is surrounded by horn blowers, drummers, and *ntsendia.*

Yes, only the men ate human flesh. Their women were never invited to these feasts. But there was one who was never invited. He was known as *nfo nkwagh* because of the scabies eating away at his entire body. The king had decreed this man be taken to the forest and left under a rock lest he contaminate the rest of his people. Scabies were not unheard of in that area, but the sight of a man's entire body, from the soles of his feet right up to the roots of his hair, overrun with scabies was unique. The festering sores on his body were not only shunned but feared. That day, when the sound of the drums started rumbling through the hills, *nfo nkwagh,* the man known as the King-of-Scabies, left the forest and was the first to arrive at the house. He brought with him a flat stone whose diameter was a little wider than the top of his head. He took a knife out of his bag, chose a spot close to the wall in a dark corner of the house, and marked the circumference of the stone on the ground with the tip of his knife. He dug a hole that could fit the size of his head and covered the hole with the stone, making sure the fit was right. He looked for a discreet corner in the house and sat down in the shadows.

The men arrived, the raffia bags holding their drinking horns slung across their chests. They were each carrying a calabash of palm wine and a Dane gun. They all sat down to laughter, drinking, singing, recounting stories of great tribal wars, of tracking and hunting expeditions. While the drinking and merriment went on, King-of-Scabies, who had been sitting unobtrusively in his dark corner, began digging through the hole until he made a passage leading to the outside. He slid through the hole, carefully surveyed his surroundings outside the house, and then slid right back into the house. No one took notice. The men were totally slewed. The palm wine had completely gone to their heads.

"Evening is fast approaching. Go and bring the meat so we can eat before it gets dark," the king slurred.

Those bound by law to carry the *bendjob* containing the victim went to get it.

"This bag is too heavy for two of us," one of the men complained.

The king sent two more men to help them. All four of them carried the *bendjob* to the sacrificial ground. The king asked the executioner to approach and receive the victim. The hand-of-death rose slowly from his seat and went and stood near the bag. One of the men opened the *bendjob. Zuuzuuu zuuzuuu, zuuzuuh!* Swarms of hungry bees flew out in droves. The first batch made straight for the door and sealed it. The rest filled the house in all directions. They angrily attacked, stung, and killed every single man in the house but one, the one man who was shunned by his peers because his skin and the skin of a pineapple seemed to share a common ancestor. Our people say that when a blind man tells you he'll stone you, you should know his foot is already on a stone. As soon as King-of-Scabies heard and saw the deadly insects, he picked up the stone from the mouth of his hole and made a hasty exit.

It is said that with all the other men dead *nfo nkwagh* went back to the palace and played the royal drum, announcing to the entire village that he was the only one at home. All the women and children flocked to the palace, where they learned of the horror now yoked to their fate for generations to come. They all converged on the house of ceremony but could not enter it. They were stunned by the truth of the calamity that had befallen them. Not one woman shed a tear. They simply collected all the oils and kerosene they could find in their homes and burned the house and its contents to ashes. The bonfire could be seen many villages away. The lone surviving male, King-of-Scabies, became king and ruled the village until his death.

Some storytellers have said that *nfo nkwagh* married all the women in the village. Some say that in the story their mothers told them *nfo nkwagh* did not become king or marry any of the women. Yet others assert that the story ends with the caution that the man who had been banished because of his condition finally came to live in the village, and all the villagers tried to pick up the pieces and build a new future. Mothers raised their children to remember but never repeat this horrific past. All I can tell you is that *ble* can always have as many plots and endings as times they are told. One thing I know for certain is that from that day men stopped eating other human beings.

My story is finished.

Pumpkin, Pumpkin, Back to the Stem

We hate it when Sun's rays burn hot on our skin. We complain when Sun hides his warmth in the folds of his face. No matter what we say, think, or do, Sun will always be a part of our lives. That's probably why Sun married one of our daughters, some say, to compensate for all the demands and anguish we've put Sun through.

This happened a long time ago. A group of women go to prepare their farms for the planting season. With the farms all cleaned up and ready for the tilling, the women sow large amounts of pumpkin seeds. They are all busy planting except one, Majieno. She spends the day roasting and eating all the pumpkin seeds she has taken to her farm. Unbeknownst to her, Mashii-the-Bird picks up some of the seeds and plants them.

Moons pass and the women decide to go on what is known as the tasting of the pumpkins. They are excited because of the thrill of sampling the first crop and the hope for signs of a good harvest. The group jokes and tells stories and laughs heartily as the women walk to their farms, but Majieno is silent throughout the trip.

"Aweh,[1] why are you so quiet? Why aren't you chatting and laughing with us?" they tease her; they poke her ribs.

[1]Friendly form of address; also, an affectionate form of address used by spouses.

"I am not feeling fine," she lies.

The women slowly ascend the last hill until they get to the flat top of the butte. From that vantage point they can all look across and see their farms on the other side. Majieno's gaze surveys her farm and it is filled with pumpkins. She suddenly whistles and laughs heartily with her friends.

"Why the sudden outburst? What tickles you so?" her friends inquire, puzzled furrows on their brows.

"The sun has touched my face at the top of this hill and I am feeling much better," she lies again.

The women each go to their respective farms. The other women busily walk around their farms and selectively pick some pumpkins. But Majieno is confronted with an inexplicable challenge. Each time she picks one pumpkin and puts it in her *neshre*, Mashii, the rightful planter, appears and commands:

Tinke bo'
Tinke bo'
Tinke tinke bo'
Back to the stem, pumpkin
Back to the stem, pumpkin
Back to the back to the stem, pumpkin

The pumpkin falls out of her *neshre* and clings to the stem. This goes on all day. In the evening the others call to her.

"Majieno, it's time to go home. Come, let's go home."

"Please come over here," Majieno beckons. "There's a bird here. When I pick a pumpkin, Mashii says, 'Back to your stem.' As you can see, the pumpkin falls out of my *neshre* and clings to the stem. All the pumpkins I've harvested today are hanging right back on the exact stems where I picked them."

"Don't worry," the women console her.

Though puzzled, they quickly contribute some pumpkins and give them to Majieno. These are the pumpkins she takes home that day. She tells her mother what has happened in the farm and her mother proposes going with her the next day.

That day, they decide on weeding instead of harvesting. When they stop and sit down to eat, Mashii flies down from the tree to eat with them. Mashii pecks on a piece of cocoyam and they offer some soup. Soon, Mashii's beak is going from cocoyam to soup, from soup to cocoyam. At the end of the meal they ask Mashii to eat the last piece of cocoyam lying in the basket. Mashii flies right in and down goes his beak on the last piece. Majieno's mother quickly turns the basket's mouth upside down and Mashii is now their captive.

"Don't kill me," Mashii begs. "I will pass out oil and salt for you."

"We will not kill you," they assure him and take him home.

From then on, Mashii produces oil or salt whenever they need it. One day, Majieno has to go to the farm, but before leaving she gives her daughter permission to ask Mashii for salt and oil when she cooks the morning meal. As soon as the girl takes Mashii into her hands, Mashii complains.

"Is that how your mother always handles me? Please hold me with tenderness."

The girl is having trouble holding Mashii with one hand and a bowl with the other. She puts down the *akekeh lah* and as she struggles to hold Mashii tenderly she opens her palm and Mashii takes flight. She spends the entire day running after Mashii but cannot catch him. She catches another bird instead. That evening, when her mother asks Mashii for oil and salt, Mashii excretes grains of sand. Majieno is so angry that she gives her daughter a beating. The girl leaves the house and sits outside, crying. Mashii hears her, comes back, and licks her tears. The girl catches Mashii, tosses him into the house to her mother, but remains outside and keeps on crying.

O sky, come down and take me
O earth, come up and take me
O sky, fall down and take me
O earth, rise up and take me

Sky and Earth tremble. The two giants fight but Earth is a bit too late. Sky swoops down and carries her away before Earth can rise up to claim her. Up up in the clouds, the girl gets married to Sun and lives with him for years. One day, she asks her mother-in-law to go *bekee* fishing with her. On their way to catch crabs, her mother-in-law confides in her.

"Whenever you want to go to Earth, you should lift this *ndeb netswegh*."[2]

"Yes, Mother."

They arrive at the river and Mother Sun stands a few steps behind her daughter-in-law. The daughter-in-law lifts a big stone and shakes it, and all the exposed crabs under it scurry for safety.

"Mother, there go the crabs. Why don't you move closer to the stone and catch them?"

As soon as Mother Sun closes in on the crabs, the girl lets go of the stone and it falls on her mother-in-law, killing her. She goes home, sits by the fireside grinding corn and singing:

Bekee bekee be kro ato ndeh neneb
Bekee bekee be kro ato ndeh neneb
Crabs crabs are eating Sun's mother's head
Crabs crabs are eating Sun's mother's head

[2]A traditional fireplace is made up of three stones acting as the tripod for pots. Selected (sometimes built) with great care, the *ndeb netswegh* is the biggest of the three and the main support stone. The subsidiary stones are replaceable, while the *ndeb netswegh* often is not. In some homes, the *ndeb netswegh* is made of bricks, built like a wall to prevent wind from blowing the flames in all directions or putting out the fire.

The girl does not know that back on earth her mother is mourning her death. She sits all day in a widow's pose, her legs stretched in front of her, tears falling freely down her face. She blames herself for her daughter's death. Ntifekwu-the-Spider sees her grief and comes to her side.

"Why cry so much?" she asks.

"I am mourning my child whom Sun came down and took away from me," Majieno stammers.

"Kill a goat for me. I will eat it and show you where your daughter is."

Majieno kills a *mbi* for Ntifekwu. Ntifekwu sits down to a good meal, after which she spins a large web. She asks Majieno to grab hold of one of the rungs and guides Majieno along. She climbs and Majieno follows her right to her daughter. The girl is overjoyed to see her mother. They spend some time together.

"I am going to see off my mother," she tells her husband on the day of Majieno's departure.

"No! I will go and escort my mother-in-law," her husband insists.

"Go then," the girl says nonchalantly to Sun.

Sun goes to see off his mother-in-law. On the way, he digs up a hole full of those terrible black *neyibobo* ants and buries her in them right up to her head. Majieno prays these be simple harmless black *li* but she soon gives up hope when sting after sting inflames her skin and begins to poison her blood.[3] The girl suspects something must have happened when her husband returns chortling wholeheartedly. She traces her husband's steps to the spot where he buried her mother. She digs her out and picks all the ants out of her hair and off her body.

"You can go back," she tells her mother. "I'll be along soon enough." Sun's wife then goes back to grinding corn and singing her song.

[3]*Li* is a generic term for ants.

Bekee bekee be kro ato ndeh neneb
Bekee bekee be kro ato ndeh neneb
Crabs crabs are eating Sun's mother's head
Crabs crabs are eating Sun's mother's head

She finishes grinding the corn, puts the flour in a bowl, places the bowl by the fireside, lifts the *ndeb netswegh,* and returns to Earth.

It is said that since she abandoned her husband, Sun has lost interest in marrying humans. We haven't heard the last from Sun, though. Every once in a while Sun reminds us of his wrath by towering over Earth and bullying us with droughts and hunger.

My story is finished.

A Secret Is Difficult to Keep

This hunter went hunting every day. He hunted even on Nshialah, the day of rest. One Nshialah he was alone in the forest when he smelled the path of a deer. A lion had also seen the deer's footprints. He was lying down on his belly, a well-sharpened axe by his side, awaiting the deer's return. The hunter looked for a hiding place but when he noticed the lion had come before him he climbed up a tree. The lion looked at the hunter, yawned, rolled over on his side, and ignored him.

The deer was away all day eating. He picked his way home as dusk was approaching. The minute the lion saw the deer he threw his axe at him but missed. The axe fell into the bushes and the lion couldn't find it. The deer immediately escaped. The lion went in search of his axe instead. The hunter sat quietly in the tree and watched the lion search from tree to tree. He would occasionally look up the tree and see the hunter still sitting there.

"Did you see the axe I flung at the deer?"

"Yes."

"Please come down and show me where it is."

"No! Your species is untrustworthy. You want me to come down so you can devour me."

"No, I will not. Please come down. I will tell you something."

"Leave this tree? I should be such a fool. I won't."

The lion persisted and the hunter finally gave in. He scaled down the tree, picked up the axe where it had fallen, and gave it to the lion.

"I will give you something in return. Aren't you here waiting for animals?"

"I am," says the hunter.

"I will reveal many things to you. When you go out hunting, you will hear the chimpanzee howl. From that moment, you will kill anything that moves on the face of the earth, but, mark you, release this secret and you die." After warning the hunter a second time, the lion gave him all the necessary instructions and libations he needed to master. They both parted ways.

From that day forth, the hunter used this power to kill many animals. When a chimpanzee howled on one hill, calling the pride to a meeting, the hunter would be there before the animals arrived. This way, he had his choice of the big game when he went hunting. One day, one of his wives asked him what made him so good at tracking big animals. The man was reluctant, not prepared to part with his secret, for he remembered the lion's warning. He joked about his strong legs instead. On another day, his wives dealt him a combined attack. They forced him to tell them his secret.

"You must have a weapon. You must tell us your hunting secret. We are your wives, not nosy strangers. You should tell us," they insisted.

Hearing the commotion was a cock searching for worms near the *nsaa*. He pecked at sand, a sign he always used to beckon his girlfriend, the hen, but the hen did not heed his call.

"Look. Listen. Why do you refuse to come when I call for you? Listen to those women. Don't you see how that man wants to tell his wives a secret between him and the lion? A secret that will end his life if they know the truth?"

The man overheard what the cock said. He jumped up like a man possessed, grabbed his cutlass, and killed his wives. Just as swiftly, he was condemned and banished from the land as custom demanded. People today still remember how late into the night piercing sounds thundered in the distance as the *kpwefo*[1] made its terrifying presence felt in this hunter's compound. No one dared step outside their homes or crack a window. Even the children had the good sense to run for their lives into neighboring homes when they heard the roaring wails of the *kpwefo* approaching their compound. The *kpwefo* leveled the entire compound to the ground. The man's name is now lost forever. It is said that from then onward, he lived alone like a thief in a foreign land, where he died alone.

That was the end of this stupid man and the end of this story.

[1]The most important, all-knowing Beba traditional regulatory society; the *kpwefo* holds the highest powers in the land. It assists the *bezofo*—the kingmakers—in crowning the new fon. Made up of *bekwob,* this body holds in check the powers of the fon and any other excesses of power. Although the *bekwob* assist the fon in his decision making, the *kpwefo* can curb or veto some of their rash or radical decisions. The *kpwefo* also possesses medicinal powers that are the strongest in the land. Among its multiple duties, the *kpwefo* carries out the sanction of putting *ngo'o* on someone's chest (see *ngo'o,* page 154, note 4).

The Test

A man had two wives, Masafi and Ajientoh. Masafi was known as the village gossip. She always had complaints for her husband whenever he came home; complaints about her co-wife: "Ajientoh is a bad wife," she'd begin. "She isn't a good cook. Ajientoh's children always bully and beat up my children. Ajientoh is selfish. Ajientoh is lazy. She spends all day at the river scrubbing her feet." It was no secret that the man loved Masafi more than Ajientoh. He had once boasted he could kill a lion for her. He bragged he'd even do something as unlawful as laying the head of the lion at her feet.[1] Ajientoh on the other hand was a quiet unassuming woman who went about her duties paying Masafi no heed. She threw herself into her daily work, performed her household chores, and bore her co-wife's insults, never telling her neglectful husband how she felt.

One day, Agha, for that was his name, woke up in a sour mood. He claimed he had a dream and in that dream it was revealed to him that his wives didn't really love him. He decided to put them to the test. It was the harvest season and Masafi and Ajientoh had left very early for their farms. Agha spent the day at home mending a hole in the goat pen. When evening

[1]A long time ago, animals such as lions, buffaloes, elephants were highly prized. A hunter lucky enough to kill one kept the meat, which he shared with family, but the head of the animal was taken to the palace and presented to the fon, who bestowed honors on the hunter.

shadows tailed across the *nsaa*, Agha caught one of the goats, slaughtered it, and removed its intestines. He lay down on his bamboo bed, next to the fireside and arranged the intestines on his bare stomach. He smeared his chest and throat with some of the goat's blood and put the cutlass he had used to butcher the animal on the floor, next to his bed.

At dusk, his wives returned from their farms with their children. They were all weighted down with heavy loads of the groundnuts, corn, and cocoyams they had harvested. Masafi was the first to rush to her husband's house to greet him. She was momentarily taken aback by the gruesome sight that awaited her. When she saw her husband lying prostrate on his bed, smeared with blood, his intestines popping out of his belly, she concluded he was dead. She took a ladder and climbed up into the ceiling. It was smoky and quite dark up there. She closed her eyes and even as she coughed, her right hand groped for the horns she knew were lying in a corner. One of the horns contained *afuondo* and the other was the horn in which her husband kept his money. She also collected other valuable items, including her husband's *ndip*. Without saying a word, Masafi took the things to her house and then left for the stream.

Ajientoh had gone straight to the stream when the women came back from the farm. After having her bath and cooking the evening meal, she went to tell Agha supper was ready. The house was as quiet and still as a grave. It was a little dark inside and she kindled the fire. The flames lit up the fireplace and she let out a piercing scream. The children heard her screams and ran to their father's house. All the neighbors rushed to the compound, wondering what misfortune could have befallen the Aghas. Ajientoh's wailing led them to Agha's bedside.

"What happened to him?"

"Oh abomination . . . Who would do such a thing?" some wondered but dared not say it out loud.

Murder was unheard of in their village and such a gruesome murder left them speechless. Who would dare spill another's blood and risk banishment from the land? The dead man's children were ushered out of the house and the room began to fill with more and more concerned neighbors. Agha's uncle, the next adult male in the line of authority, took charge and began issuing orders about the cleansing and burial rituals that had to be performed. But before he could issue any more directives, Agha jumped up from his bed, silencing his uncle. The intestines fell to the ground, splattering blood on some of the onlookers. Women screamed, some people took to their heels, some fled, telling their neighbors they had seen a ghost in Agha's compound.

"My brothers. My sisters," Agha raised his hands, reassuring them he was not dead. "My people, what you're seeing are the entrails of a goat. When you don't understand the language of the drum you say it is noise. Had I not died, I would not have known which of my wives truly loves me."

When Masafi heard these words, she took her things, as the Beba say, and fled to her father's compound, never to return. Agha's neighbors shunned him for what they saw as a cruel joke. Some called him a coward; a man with no testicles between his thighs. To continue living in their village Agha had to atone for what he had done. He bought five jugs of palm wine, cooked two bunches of plantain, invited his neighbors, and begged their forgiveness. They ate, drank, and poured libation in front of his house. Only then did Ajientoh agree to remain his wife.

The story is finished.

The Sacred Door

So, this is how it is. It's all about a poor man. His father and his mother die, leaving him with nothing. He has no crops in his farm. Not one young woman will look at him or think of marrying him. Some call him the village scarecrow. For that reason he often flees to the forest where he spends most of his days. No one actually knows what he does among the trees. One day, he takes his cutlass and axe and goes into the forest to look for a fertile piece of land to plant his seeds. Not confident of the parts of the forest he already knows, he decides to go even further and deeper into the forest. He gets tired and sits down under a mahogany tree. After a while he feels strong hunger pains; his stomach wambles, he feels faint but he has no food. He searches the trees hoping to find some fruits. There are none in sight. To his surprise he sees an old woman instead. He greets her, "Mother are you lost?"

She says, "Where are you from?"

The man says, "Father-Mine and Mother-Mine have died. I am looking for a place to plant some seeds."

And he hears her command, "Give me that cutlass and axe."

He gives her the cutlass and the axe he is carrying across his shoulder.

The old woman says, "Turn around. Take off your clothes."

The man turns around, his back to the old woman. He takes off his brown tattered singlet and the loincloth tied around his waist. He finishes undressing, looks up, and finds himself in a different country. People of this country are happy to see him. They take him to their palace and crown him as their king. The poor man can hardly believe what is happening to him. A *nkwob*, the most senior of all the nobles, gives the king a tour of the entire palace. There is a lot to see: all the living quarters, the ceremonial grounds, the king's gardens. It takes all day. It is a long day. They finally come to a door and the *nkwob* bows and says, "Mbeh, everything in this palace is yours, but you should never open this door. It is the sacred door."

Years pass. The king settles comfortably into his duties. He looks after his subjects. He is doing a very good job. His subjects love him and the gods bless him with many offspring. But, as the Beba say, the king's throat is bitter, very bitter inside. He is unhappy about the door. "Why shouldn't I touch that door? Am I not the king? Have I not been good to my people? Why am I being treated as if I were a stranger? What is it about that door?" He gnashes his teeth. The sacred door torments his dreams. He vows to do something about it—after all, *he* is the king.

His plan materializes on the most important day of the year, the day of the *nwa ngeh*, the Feast of the Cutting-of-the-Grass. The king gives food; he gives drinks to his subjects. The people are festive. They *nwa ngeh* and invoke their gods. They thank their gods for the rains, for the new births, for good health, for the bountiful harvest, for another peaceful year. They pour libations, kill a goat, spill its blood, and say incantations to ward off their enemies, bad omens, and evildoers. They eat and drink and dance and celebrate. The festivities over, the king tries unsuccessfully to fall asleep. His satiated subjects have stumbled unto their beds and are profoundly asleep. One lonely figure begins to roam the halls of the palace. He can hear his tortured mind whispering into the darkness, "Today is the day I must open that door. If I don't open it on a sacred day like this, the annual day of reckoning, when can I? A sacred day like this one merits the opening of the sacred door." The king tiptoes through the graveyard silence of the palace. He approaches the door and gently opens it. He steps outside and shuts the door. He suddenly feels shivers shoot down his spine. He realizes there are no clothes on his body. He is stark naked. The old woman is there, sitting under the mahogany tree.

"Here are your things," she says, handing him his rags, his cutlass, and his axe.

What would you have done?

The story is finished.

Hunting Elephants

At the time when our story begins, Adieh is known as the best elephant hunter in the village. He owns a scraggy, bad-tempered-looking dog. That scrawny, rangy dog is worth more than an army of good hunting dogs. This cantankerous dog eats a lot but always looks as thin as cattle grazing on sparse hills in the dry season. Adieh makes sure he always carries the right quantities of food when they both go hunting, especially hunting elephants.

These elephant-hunt expeditions are few and far between but are beneficial to the entire village. On the eve of an important celebration in the village, Adieh takes his dog hunting. But before they leave, he cooks a lot of fufu-corn and bitter-leaf soup for the dog. This dog would not cross two streams or climb two hills without asking for food. Adieh dutifully feeds him.

They finally arrive at the hunting ground and the dog asks his master to hide behind the trunk of a huge mahogany tree.

"Let all the fat elephants go by. Wait until you see the last one that looks as skinny as me. Shoot that one," the dog instructs his master, climbs up a tree, and starts playing enchanting music with his *nelo*.

minser da ko'o
mimfo mimfo

mimfo de ko'o
minser minser

When elephants approach
buffaloes buffaloes
When buffaloes approach
elephants elephants

Adieh sees the elephants stride majestically toward him. The first behemoths crush plants and trees with every step. Adieh watches them rumble by with an attentive expert hunter's eye. Huge elephants, moderately big ones, small ones, thin ones follow in succession. Any other hunter would have opened fire at such a sight but Adieh is more than a good hunter, he is an obedient master as well. At last, he spots the skinny elephant at the end of the procession, waits till it draws level with him and *twaaah!* he shoots it. *Kpwuum!* the elephant falls down dead and so do all the elephants that have gone before it. Adieh takes his dog home and returns with some of the villagers. They butcher the elephants and carry all the meat home. The meat is shared and some is used for a thanksgiving celebration.

Time passes and Adieh's younger brother is going to take a wife. He desperately wants to prove to his in-laws he is worth his salt. Manoji goes to his brother and asks for his dog. As a hunter, Manoji is nothing compared to his brother. He has no hunting talent whatsoever. Adieh knows this but he cannot say no to his brother. He reluctantly offers Manoji his dog. "Give the dog as much food and as many times as he asks for it," Adieh warns his brother. Manoji does not heed his brother's warning. He complains and curses the dog even though he only feeds the dog thrice. As you can imagine, the dog does not eat one-third of what it normally consumes on such trips with his master.

"Do not shoot the first animal you see. Wait until you see the last one that is as skinny as I am before you shoot," the dog instructs Manoji and climbs up the tree. He signals to Manoji to hide behind a huge tree trunk.

minser da ko'o
mimfo mimfo
mimfo de ko'o
minser minser

When elephants are rising
buffaloes buffaloes
When buffaloes are rising
elephants elephants

Good God! Is Manoji witnessing a miracle or is this really an elephant? He has never seen anything so gigantic before. He is trembling all over like a leaf in an August rain-storm. That first elephant stomps by, then a second, and a third, and Manoji can hold back no longer. "Why should I wait for a skinny one when humongous beasts are within my reach?" he chides himself. No longer able to restrain himself, he raises his double-barrel, aims and *twaaah* shoots the elephant. The first three elephants fall down dead but the rest stampede back the way they have come. Wild winds whirl in the surrounding area and a storm immediately breaks, shaking the entire forest. Trees are uprooted; branches are ripped from trees and flung in every direction. Worse, strong winds lift the dog from the branch on which it is clinging for safety and fling the dog into a pool of murky water. Manoji searches for the dog in vain and goes home to report the loss to Adieh. Adieh is furious and will hear none of it. He asks his brother to go back to the forest and not return without his dog.

Manoji summons to the forest all the known experts in the land who dabble in the occult. Herbalists and diviners come from every hill and valley and hamlet. They are bent on flaunting their knowledge of the leaves, the moons, and ancestral wisdom. For eight days and eight nights, from Nkpezah to Ntobah to Ndzembebeh to Ndokuh to Nshialah to Webloh to Bamidzetoh to Bamikoh, they all try, but none of them is successful in their bid to free the dog. Adieh then makes an announcement: "Whoever brings my dog back by the next Nshialah, the day when the land and the people rest, will be handsomely rewarded."

For four days the experts rest. On Nshialah people flock to the pool. No one would dare miss the spectacle everyone expects the medicine men would reserve for this final show. Some of the plant-and-root experts throw herbs into the pool; others pronounce invocations lay people can hardly understand; some chant incantations never before heard in the village and beyond. Still no dog in sight. All this fruitless drama, yielding no results. Adieh is about to give up when a man rises to his feet, to hushed voices. He is thin, his clavicles stick out, and his feet are completely infested with jiggers. Some comment that he resembles the scrawny dog. Most do not find the joke funny. Onlookers watch this man with skepticism and even scorn. If experts have tried and failed, what can this diminutive man do? But they step aside; they make way for him as the man cautiously approaches the pool holding a twig in his hand. He holds the twig to his lips, whispers inaudible words, and plunges the twig into the pool. When he pulls the twig out of the pool, the dog is clinging to it. A roar goes up in the forest. Adieh is reunited with his dog and the man claims his reward. A grateful Adieh takes his dog home. Manoji becomes the laughingstock of the village, most especially of his future in-laws.

This story is finished.

Afterword

My earliest impressions of Cameroon were gleaned from the stories I was told by older people. Their comments revolved around two things: first, that Mount Cameroon—also known as Mount Fako, the Throne of Thunder, and the Chariot of the Gods—the highest peak in West and Central Africa, is the site of the earliest recorded volcanic eruption in the region; and second, that the country they call home was named after prawns by some white people. It is said that in the fifth century BCE, while sailing along the Atlantic coast of West Africa, Hanno, the Carthaginian explorer and ship's captain, observed Mount Cameroon erupting and inscribed in his travel writings the name *Theon Ochema*, Chariot of the Gods. He is said to have noted that the fires from the mountain were so hot and so bright that the flames reached up and touched the stars. Firm believers in this historical version point out that Mount Cameroon (also called Mount Fako because it is situated in Fako Division of the South West Province) is the only active volcano on the coast of West Africa, erupting seven times in the twentieth century alone.[1] They also point to the fact that the mountain is known locally as *monga-ma loba*—Seat of the Gods.

I was born in the South West Province but was raised through my teenage years in the grasslands of the North West Province, where Beba, my village of origin, is situated. Mount Cameroon has therefore always held a kind of mystery for me.

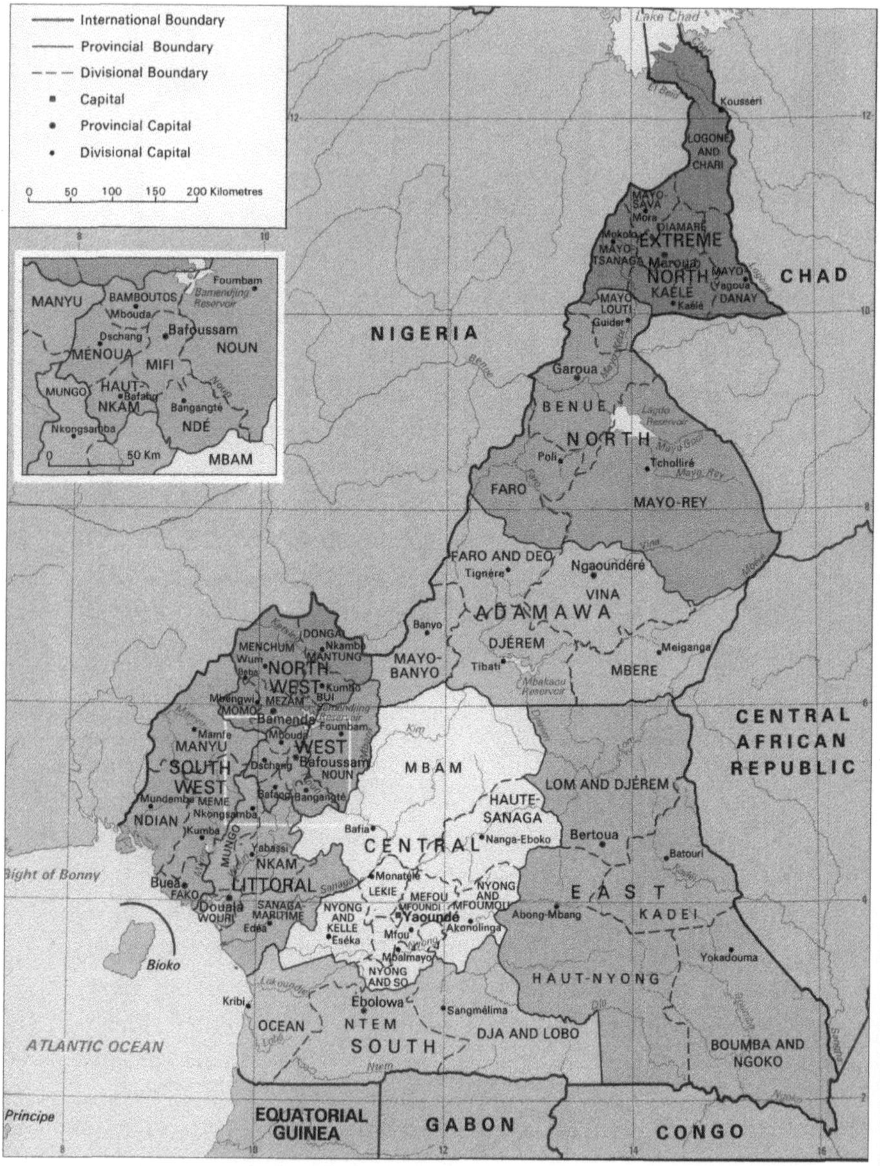

Cameroon—Administrative. Map taken from *Macmillan School Atlas for Cameroon* © Macmillan Publishers Ltd. 1985. Reproduced with permission.

As a young girl, I was fascinated with these stories of the so-called discovery by Hanno, of flaming arrows reaching for the stars, and with the fact that Debundscha, the wettest place on the African continent and the place with the second-highest rainfall in the world, lies at the foot of the Seat/Chariot of the Gods. I found it amusing that my country was named after big juicy shrimp, and by a bunch of white men we did not know. I could not grasp what that act of naming really entailed, but the teachers who taught me in primary school and the adults who told us those stories by the evening fire were not amused. They insisted that branding us with the name of shrimp was an invitation to a feast. The metaphor was lost on my young sensibilities.

As I got older and attended primary and secondary school, our curriculum was tailored to the British education system of O levels and A levels. In our history lessons, little was afforded the various peoples who migrated to and now inhabit the sahel and plauteau regions of the mostly Muslim north, or the grasslands, littoral, and forest regions of the largely Christian south. History lessons were dominated by European and Cameroon's colonial history. Only later, at the University of Yaounde, did I, on my own, read all the books I could find that addressed the various kingdoms, chiefdoms, and indigenous civilizations of the people who today call Cameroon home.[2]

Cameroon: A Brief History

In the fifteenth century, the Portuguese navigator Fernao Do Poo and his crew were so taken by the sheer quantity of *mbea towè* in the Wouri estuary in Douala that they named the river *Rio dos Camarões*, River of Prawns.[3] But this name was to undergo further changes with each new arrival of European traders (in both natural and human resources) and conquerors. The name became Camarones to the Spaniards, Kamerun to the

Germans, the Cameroons to the British, and Cameroun to the French. The Portuguese arrived in the fifteenth century, launched sugar plantations, and began the slave trade in the sixteenth century. The Dutch were hot on their heels and took over the slave trade from the Portuguese in the seventeenth century. Only later did the Germans begin the effective colonization of German Kamerun, a fact Germany consolidated at the Berlin Conference (1884–85) with the partition of Africa. The country known today as La République du Cameroun/Republic of Cameroon was to endure numerous political and geographical facelifts before it gained its right to self-government in 1958 and independence in 1960.

Cameroon is the only African nation to have been colonized by three European nations—Germany, Britain, and France. The groundwork for this colonial legacy began with the late nineteenth-century scramble for and partition of Africa by European powers. The Berlin Conference effectively legitimized German colonial authority over Cameroon. Germany cemented its control with two treaties: one with Douala chiefs in 1884 establishing the German Protectorate of Kamerun; and the other in 1885 with the British, who handed over control of the Southern Cameroons, to be administered as part of the German Protectorate of Kamerun. Things would change in the early twentieth century with Germany's defeat in World War I. British and French forces took hold of the Cameroon territory; the Northern Cameroons and the Southern Cameroons went to Britain, and the rest of the territory to France. In 1922, a League of Nations mandate reaffirmed Britain's control over the Northern and the Southern Cameroons and French control over the remaining territory. The British and French mandate would later be renewed as UN trusteeships after World War II, in 1946, a time when resistance to colonialism gained momentum and spread throughout the African continent.

The struggle for independence resulted in French Cameroun gaining the right to self-government in 1958 and independence in 1960. This newly independent francophone state became La République du Cameroun, with Ahmadou Ahidjo as its president. The fate of the British Cameroons was decided on February 11, 1961, by a UN-sponsored plebiscite. The British Northern Cameroons joined Nigeria, while the Southern Cameroons chose cohabitation with La République du Cameroun. After constitutional negotiations, these two entities became the Federal Republic of Cameroon on October 1, 1961. Even so, Ahmadou Ahidjo could not exercise the total control he desired over this federated state. He crushed political insurgency by opposition parties, reminiscent of the 1958 assassination of anticolonial nationalist leaders such as Ruben Um Nyobé. He cemented his power by introducing the one-party system under the umbrella of his party, the Union Nationale Camerounaise (Cameroon National Union) in 1966, and declared a unitary state in 1972 known as La République Unie du Cameroun/United Republic of Cameroon. When Ahidjo's successor, Paul Biya, took over in 1982, he would by decree in 1984 once again change the name to La République du Cameroun/Republic of Cameroon. This name holds political implications harkening back to the pre-plebiscite, pre-federation era and is therefore heavily contested and even rejected by secessionist movements seeking independence for the former British Southern Cameroons.[4]

Official Bilingualism

Ahmadou Ahidjo sought to consolidate his power by getting rid of the federation and manufacturing a "united republic." Among his many policies was the institutionalization of official bilingualism (English and French were declared and still are Cameroon's official languages). This policy of bilingualism was most evident at the University of Yaounde, the lone state university and main center of higher learning for three decades.[5] It is noteworthy that almost five decades after independence, most state institutions are known by their French acronyms, sometimes presented with accompanying English translations but often without. French dominates the language of public discourse. At the University of Yaounde, anglophone professors tended to teach their courses in English while their francophone counterparts taught their courses in French, regardless of whether a class was made up of anglophones, francophones (which was more often the case), or both. Clearly, in a system serving a population comprising an 80 percent French-speaking majority and a 20 percent English-speaking minority, the policy of official bilingualism was less demanding of and for the francophone majority.[6] It also meant that anglophone students received most of their instruction in French. (Consequently, English-speaking Cameroonians—whether educated or not—have been, de facto, the most bilingual Cameroonians.) The anglophone minority would not reap the true benefits assured by this policy. Disillusioned, many chose to go to Nigeria or other English-speaking countries in West and East Africa (such as Ghana, Sierra Leone, Kenya, Tanzania), Europe, and North America to pursue university studies.

Publishing in Cameroon was similarly dominated by the French language, by foreign publishing houses, and especially by French publishers. Theoretically, Ahidjo and later Biya emphasized the need for local autonomous publishing, which was "purported to lead to cultural independence and to contribute to nation-building. Cultural independence and nation-building are two concepts which acquire a particular significance in the French ex-colonies, where the cultural aspect of the colonization process was dominant."[7] Such "promotion of cultural independence, and especially of cultural autonomy from Cameroon's major former colonial master, France" was commendable, and the few local publishers who were energized by cultural aspirations tried to take up the challenge, yet stringent government policies themselves made it almost impossible for such publishing or contributions to Cameroon literature to thrive.[8]

Ironically, this was happening at a time in the 1960s through the 1980s when Cameroon was touted as a cultural Mecca, often referred to as *l'Afrique en miniature*—Africa-in-miniature—and for good reason. Éditions CLÉ in Yaounde was the first publishing house in Africa, founded by Protestant missionaries in 1963 as a religious publishing house. CLÉ began publishing fiction by African authors in 1967 and the Who's Who of francophone writing. (The creation of the Nouvelles Éditions Africaines in Dakar in 1972 would later reinforce the publishing network enjoyed by francophone writers and scholars.) In his essay "The Development of Book Publishing" in *Journalism and Mass Communication in Africa: Cameroon*, Julius Che Tita notes:

> The publishing industry in Cameroon is in transition because of the reformation of Centre d'Edition et de Production pour l'Enseignement et la Recherche (CEPER). Originally known as Centre de Production de Manuel[s et d'Auxiliaires de l'Enseignement] (CEPMAE) it was established by UNESCO in 1972 to produce teaching manuals for the central African region. The Cameroon government took it over in 1977 when the participating countries failed to honor their financial obligations. CEPER was in charge of producing textbooks, which had been approved by the Ministry of National Education. It was not allowed to stray into general literature despite the profitability of textbook production. CEPER personified the negative side of state participation in publishing. The strong position of the Ministry of National Education reduced CEPER to a mere printing press. As a result of government policy and failures, CEPER was sold in 1992. . . .
>
> Another big player in the publishing scene in Cameroon is Editions CLE that stands out as the leading publisher of general literature in Cameroon and the whole of Francophone Africa.

> Editions CLE has survived the scourges of African publishing first because of its strong financial and editorial base as well as its association with the church. By 2001, it had over 500 titles in its list and has gradually been shifting from its religious roots to all types of publishing. CEPER and CLE are among the leading publishing houses in Cameroon. (68)

Sadly, the international and well-deserved reputation enjoyed by francophone Cameroon writers eluded their anglophone compatriates at home. Éditions CLÉ did not publish in English. Anglophone Cameroon writers and scholars had to go to Nigeria or the West to publish their books. Most could not afford to do that. Some resorted to self-publishing up to a few hundred copies of their work, which they hawked themselves. All the while, Éditions CLÉ publicized its participation in the preservation of Cameroon's cultural heritage with the publication of volumes of oral narratives in French.[9] Most collections of Cameroon folktales or oral literature in English are buried in master's theses and doctoral dissertations produced by graduate students of the Department of Negro-African Literature at the University of Yaounde.[10] The few published collections in English either are out of print or difficult to locate in bookstores or databases because the limited quantity in which self-published collections are printed makes their availability in bookstores sporadic and inconsistent. Indeed, it is often only by coincidence that one is able to buy such books directly from the author or occasionally through a lucky find at a newspaper stand or a street vendor's.

The Beba

Beba is situated in Menchum Division, the largest division in the North West Province.[11] Menchum Division is made up principally of Upper Fungom, Lower Fungom, Aghem, Kom, Bum,

Essimbi, and Beba-Befang. Compared with the other geographical groups, Beba-Befang is peculiar because of its name, area, and cultural practices. In his 1978 D.E.S. (Diplôme d'Études Supérieures) thesis, "A Geographical Appraisal of the Rural Development Process in Beba-Befang," Fidelis A. Afuba notes: "The name Beba-Befang is a combination of names of two villages: Beba at the extreme South West and Befang at the extreme North East of the tribe. All the other villages fall within the tribe whether their cultural traits are similar or not. Even the two villages whose combination has been adopted have no cultural or ethnic similarities" (49).[12]

Situated in the southwest corner of Menchum Division, Beba-Befang shares a boundary with Mezam, Momo, and Manyu to the south and the west. Essimbi and Aghem are located to the northeast. Essimbi is inhabited primarily by the Essimbis, the two Fungoms by the Fungoms, Aghem by the Aghems, and Kom primarily by the Bikom. Beba-Befang does not possess such cultural homogeneity. It comprises six villages: Beba, Batomo, Okoromanjang, Mukuru, Modele, and Befang.[13] Clearly, Beba-Befang was a political delimitation created for administrative convenience.[14] However, even today, a Beba would have to emphasize that s/he is from the Beba-Befang area for a geopolitical connection to be made and understood.[15]

The Beba have as their neighbors Konda, Oshie, Bako, Batomo, Okoromanjang, Otang, Mundum, and Bafut. Beba village is made up of the following quarters: Soka, Mbekuyam, Mbebatebeh, Bango, Bafui, Sanoh, Mbruneluh, Mualah, Ntsoboh, Mbamba, Nta Bezah, Mbenstah, Shisong, Fombe, and Aga. The area abounds in slopes, hills, valleys, rivers, streams, and springs. It is a regular phenomenon to have to go down a hill, cross a stream, and climb yet another hill when trekking from one quarter—and sometimes, from one compound—to another. Rains are heavy in the rainy season, and the rivers and streams rush down their slopes, brawling over stony beds.

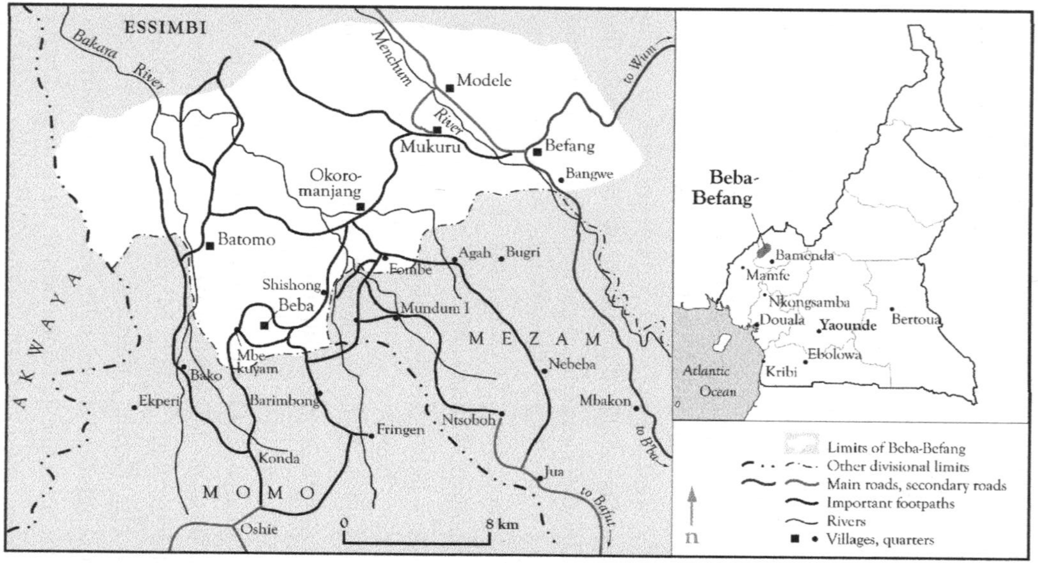

The Beba-Befang Clan. The inset map shows the location of Beba-Befang in Cameroon. Adapted from Fidelis Afuba's 1978 D.E.S. thesis, "A Geographical Appraisal of the Rural Development Process in Beba-Befang."

These rivers and streams are shallow in the dry season and some of the springs dry up. However, the dry season does not last long, and when the rains return there is a general and rapid recovery of life. "Secondary deciduous forest covers almost the whole of Beba. In fact, according to elders, fifty or more years ago, Beba was covered by thick semi-deciduous forest. But much deforestation and later fallowing in the process of shifting cultivation resulted in the regeneration of a secondary deciduous forest composed of moderated trees and tall grass" (Afuba, 68). Reminiscent of these deciduous forests are clusters of huge trees and palm trees that dominate the landscape. Beba's forests and sandy loam soils are rich in organic residue that favor this farming and agrarian community.

Origin and Migration of the Beba

The Beba have stories explaining phenomena or important sociocultural activities such as the *nwa ngeh*—the ritual Cutting-of-the-Grass Festival—intertribal wars, and chieftancy succession conflicts. Inevitably, one such story is about the origin, migration, and settlement at the present site. As narrated to me in 1980 by Fidelis Afuba, the Beba are of Widikum origin. The people maintain that a large ship came and anchored and all the various groups of Widikum origin came ashore and migrated, generally northward. (Afuba noted that there is some faint relationship here between this "natural ship" and the fact that the Cross River is navigable up to Mamfe. The actual correlation between the two phenomena is a subject worthy of research.) The Beba moved north to Batibo and northwest into present-day Menemoland (Mbengwi and Njindom in Momo Division). Tribal wars kept the migrating group on the move until there was settlement at Nta Metshie around Njimaya in western Bafut. Here the Beba lived in collaboration with the

Bafut, a people of the Mundum group.[16] Skilled in blacksmithing, the Beba made weapons such as spears, cutlasses, and knives, and quickly established their hegemony over the Bafut, Mbakong, Otang, Bugri, and Mundum I. However, their influence was checked to the north by the Menchum River. Across the river, the Aghem had established their supremacy over the people of Befang and the surrounding villages. The Beba were ruled at this time by Adieh Yiboh, the first Beba fon from whom continuous genealogy can be traced.

Soon after settlement at Nta Metshie, a tragic event befell the Beba. The larger group of the Bafut arrived from Ndop and invaded the Bafut and the Beba. The former were victorious and Adieh Yiboh was taken captive to the palace of Bafut. It is said that this prisoner of war was treated with all the rights attendant to his status as a fon. In the meantime, the defeated Beba moved westward to a place called Bwam Bwam. But Adieh Yiboh fell sick in captivity. The story goes that a Bali man, known to be a diviner and reputed magician, told the fon the Bafut would perish if the Beba fon died in captivity. This prophecy led to Adieh Yiboh's release. He reunited with his people at Bwam Bwam and promptly confiscated all their weapons to avert further wars. But one citizen hid his spear. Soon after Adieh's release and at the request of the fon of Bafut, the Aghem attacked unarmed Beba people. Many were killed and many more were captured. But while the Aghem prince was leading the captives away, the man who had hidden his spear dashed out of the bush and killed the prince, and all the captives escaped. Many Beba dispersed to Mandankwe, Kom, and other areas in the Bamenda region after their battles with the Bafut and the Aghem. Those who chose not to flee later assembled and moved back to Ntah Metshie around Akofunguba in Bafut.

Angobe, the prince and destined heir of Adieh Yiboh, used to go southwestward into Batomo and Okoromanjang and present-day Beba to hunt. When his father died around 1898, Angobe became fon and moved southwestward to Batomo, taking the few Beba living in Ntah Metshie with him. The Batomo gave Angobe and his people some land. With the tools they produced from blacksmithing they greatly improved the lives of the indigenous Batomo: knives the Beba made replaced the burning method the Batomo used for shaving; spears and Dane guns replaced stones and clubs for hunting.

With time, the Beba population began to increase rapidly, thanks to both a rise in the birthrate and the return of the self-exiled. The Batomo grew alarmed by this demographic shift and wanted to wage war against the Beba. But the Batomo women who valued the advantages of their association and harmonious living with the Beba opposed this war. The Beba believe they would have been victorious because they were more skilled in the use of their superior weapons. Angobe continued to hunt buffalo, deer, antelope, and other animals at the present Beba site. Around 1901, a majority of the Beba who had scattered during the Bafut/Aghem wars returned to this site. Not long afterward, the Beba began wars of expansion against the Batomo, Bako, Mundum, and Okoromanjang. Many quarters in present-day Beba are named after their former inhabitants, for instance, Mbe-Kanji (forest of the Okoromanjang people), Nta-Bandep (hill of the Mundum people), Mbe-Batebe (forest of the Batomo people).

Agha Nefo succeeded his father. He was reputed to have many young wives. Princes were known to woo the fon's wives, and this caused friction in the palace. When Agha Nefo had knowledge of such behavior, he would place the stem of a plantain tree in front of the house of the wanton prince as a signal to the prince to leave the palace—in other words, the prince was exiled. A bitter succession dispute raged among the princes at their father's disappearance (the Beba never say, "The fon has died"; he is said to have disappeared or to be lost—meaning the people have lost their ruler). Rather than be subordinate to another, some of the princes left the palace and settled elsewhere in Beba. Prince Asanji, however, went much farther away, taking his followers with him to what is known today as Bombe, a place of level lands, located in Manyu Division. Though Bombe is a full day's trek from Beba and one would have to travel through other villages and language groups to get there, the people of Bombe consider themselves Beba despite not being "ruled" by the fon of Beba. They speak Beba; relatives visit both ways between Beba and Bombe; and they still maintain and perform Beba celebratory and ritual practices. The ruler of the people of Bombe might refer to himself as a fon—after all, his male ancestor was a breakaway prince who founded his own fondom—but this prince (and his subsequent heirs) is not regarded by the Beba as a fon; rather, he is always referred to as a prince of the fondom of Beba.[17]

Beba Social Organization

The Beba are organized according to four big family groups called *mekro* (singular, *nekro*) the *Bafih*, the *Banjir*, the *Batolah*, and the *Bantrialah*. Among the Beba, "*be*" means "people." However, the prefix *ba* means those, those people, people of. *Bafih:* those who are there, that is, right here. *Banjir:* those who are across, over there: one descends a hill, crosses a stream, strides along a valley, ascends a hill, and the *Banjir* are over there, up the hill. They are across, over that way. The *Batolah* are the people who live up there, on the upper side, one might infer the northern part of the land. Similarly, the *Bantrialah* are those who live down there; on the lower side, one might infer the southern part of the land.

A *nekro* embodies all who share a common father or ancestor. Each *nekro* is made up of families and their subfamilies.

The *Bafih nekro* families are the Bangoh, Baro, Bafih. The *Banjir* families are the Bantah, Bonefeh, Bafuke, Mbenti, Bengesoh, Befui, Batobeh, Boyiko, Botaka. The *Batolah* families are the Bomah, Boyibo, Batolah, Bo Adieh Yiboh, Bodestere, Bazo, Bodieh, Bomeko, Bodoh; and the *Bantrialah* families are the Besongwere, Besongui, Boyitswe, Boyikah.[18] All the members of a *nekro* are not necessarily agglomerated in one geographical location. *Mekro* are patrilineal and exogamous.[19] Families are spread throughout Beba and in other parts of Cameroon but the people know their *mekro* and stick to them especially for family rituals, public negotiations, and cultural celebrations.

The royal family currently belongs in the *Batolah nekro* in general and the *Batolah* family in particular. Fondeh Henry Angobe II, the current fon of Beba, who is referred to simply as *Nfo*, rules over all the *mekro*. It is his duty to solve all the problems that are brought before him by his citizens or find acceptable methods of conflict resolution within or outside the village. He is assisted in these tasks by *bekwob* (nobles) and *bejindia*[20] (heads of families; they can also be quarter heads). These men act as advisers to the fon and help communicate his wishes to the people. The fon's messages to the people are delivered throughout the land by royal messengers, pages, or retainers known as *nstendia*. In precolonial times, the fon could exercise absolute power of final decision making and management of village affairs. Such powers made fons and chiefs invaluable allies of colonial administrations. They oversaw the collection of taxes and the exploitation of manual labor and natural resources. Although the fon's powers are restricted in contemporary times, when the need arises, he is still relied on by the postcolonial administrative authority. The fon, therefore, can no longer wield absolute power. Sometimes, citizens dissatisfied with his judgment have been known to take their cases to Wum, the capital and administrative seat of Menchum Division, to seek justice within the modern court system. Some do get satisfaction there while some have seen their cases referred back to the fon—customary law and civil law coexist in the Cameroon judicial system. The fon has thus become an instrument employed by the state to execute administrative and political decisions. It is not uncommon for the fon to be involved with such matters as the collection of taxes, development projects, or the organization of elections.

Storytelling among the Beba

In the last three decades, the practice of storytelling has undergone changes within Beba communities, depending on whether one lives in the village or in an urban area. Rural exodus, for whatever reasons, has over the years gradually changed the way the Beba people relate to their culture and oral traditions.[21] The Beba still indulge in storytelling in the village, but the frequency with which *ble* are told has dramatically reduced in urban areas. When I was a graduate student at the University of Yaounde, I used to visit relatives in Yaounde, Douala, and the CDC camps. Sometimes, I'd beg to hear one story or another. It was not unusual for a relative to respond: "Do I remember them anymore?" "Do we tell *ble* anymore? We get so tired from this (plantation) work, who has the time to tell *ble* when we come home?" "Ah, you have come with your funny questions again." They'd joke that a drop of water does not swell the banks of *nki Mbu* but there'd be no river without that drop of water either and then proceed to tell me the story I had requested.[22]

Meaning and Categorization of *Ble*

The Beba use the term *ble* (plural; *a-ble*, singular) to mean *stories;* however, *ble* is also an all-encompassing term used to describe Beba oral narratives in particular and Beba oral literature in general. Scholars of folklore, of (African) oral literature, and specifically (African) oral/prose narratives have wrestled with the difficulty of categorizing oral narratives.[23] Okpewho notes four problematic categories that for a long time have served as the basis for categorization: "the obvious protagonist of the tale" (181); "the purpose revealed in the content"; "the characteristic quality of the tale"; and "context or occasion" (182). Categorizing oral narratives using these markers is problematic because one story can fall into more than one category. For example, most of the *ble* in part 1 are etiological tales, tales that explain why this or that phenomenon has come to be the way it is today; they can be referred to as explanatory tales. Though most characters in these stories are animals with clearly anthropomorphic traits, one can easily select tales in part 2 and part 3, albeit with real human characters, that could similarly be described as explanatory tales: "The Flutes" for one, explains the origin of diseases in the universe; "King-of-Scabies" explains why cannibalism is a thing of the past. However, on closer examination, they are much more than that. "The Flutes" is also about human foibles and explores the complex relationship between envy, greed, gender, sexuality, polygamy, and power relations. "King-of-Scabies" can also be described as a legend, a story that seeks to capture a pseudo-historical event or time when cannibalism might have been a reality. That this story is not set in Beba and that the language of the song in the story is not Beba is very revealing. It forces the (Beba) listener to ask such questions as: Does this mean cannibalism was practiced among a people the Beba knew during their period of migration to their present location? Did a contemporary neighboring people practice cannibalism? Did the Beba themselves practice cannibalism or did they so abhor it in others that they created this story to warn against it? Was this story created by another people and the Beba made it part of their *ble?*[24] Many fables that are sometimes referred to as "dilemma tales" pose a dilemma and provide a solution to that dilemma, for instance, "Union Is Strength," "The Huntress," "The Test"; however, "The Sacred Door" is a dilemma tale that is better described as a fable because it poses the question, "What would you have done?" and leaves the answer to each member of the audience. Further, how would one categorize the story "Penis, Testicles, and Vagina"? Is it a simple explanatory tale that seeks to elucidate a biological phenomenon, is it a dilemma tale that poses a difficult choice for each of the protagonists, or is it a fable that imaginatively forces the audience to think about mundane but important issues and values that govern human lives such as greed, selfishness, generosity, and love, to name a few? I am suggesting that the Beba term *ble* aptly captures the overlapping and blurred boundaries that govern oral narratives.[25] That is why even though *ble* must be understood as a generic term for Beba oral literature and Beba oral narratives in particular, inherent in *ble* are subgenres that make up the fullness of what the term *ble* connotes. Myths, legends, and folktales are also referred to as *ble.* These *ble* are infused with proverbs, songs, chants, riddles, tongue-twisters, idioms; with formulaic phrases, dialogue, repetition, digression, ideophones such as onomatopoeia, exclamation, imagery, symbolism, and so on, depending on the storyteller and the narrative structure or techniques s/he chooses to employ during performance.[26] Folktales are the most popular and are referred to as *ble,* meaning stories. Specific nomenclature is reserved for proverbs, which are known as *bone di—bone* meaning sayings and *di* meaning the original, the first language; one must be competent in that language to use proverbs. Proverbs are also designated as *atop akop*—language that is known by *beh kop* because the meanings are "hidden" and one must "dig deep," one must belong to the group of *beh kop,*[27] for proverbs are the art of the elders, of those who have put themselves through a rigorous apprenticeship in the art of manipulating language and rhetorical speech.

Function of Oral Narratives among the Beba

Ble are told by everyone and especially by women. Storytelling usually takes place in the evening when children and adults have returned home after a hard day's work. Dirty and tired, they take their evening baths, most often in the river. Sometimes, children haul water from the river for others to bathe at home. Refreshed, they sit around the evening fire and tell stories while performing other activities such as shucking corn or shelling groundnuts, *egusi* (pumpkin seeds), beans, or peas for making *koki*. Generally, they share *ble* to pass the time, but they share *ble*, sing songs, and test their wit for relaxation as well as for entertainment. Storytellers not only spin imaginative dramas for the listener-participants but also employ language and narrative techniques that later serve as a rhetorical framework for communication outside the context of storytelling. Storytellers narrate *ble* to impart lessons about Beba society (for *ble* are an invaluable conduit of cultural education about their people and their neighbors) as well as creation myths and legends that historically ground the children in their environment and related geographical region.

It is not uncommon to hear a woman discipline a child by making a direct reference to *a-ble*. *Ble* therefore have functions at the general but also at the individual, and specifically gendered, level. My mother for instance often navigated both. For one, she was a mother of ten. When a child would throw a tantrum, rebel, and flat-out refuse to do a chore, my mother would often say, "Do you remember what happened to the boy/girl who . . . ?" Or she'd state bluntly, "If you don't do this, then what happened to so-and-so will happen to you. Mark my words." Further, I was raised in a strict Catholic family dominated by lessons and rules of good (Christian) conduct. My mother clearly saw a convergence between Beba and Christian mores, which she adapted in her mothering duties. None worked harder than my mother when we labored all day in the farm hoeing or weeding or harvesting crops such as groundnuts, beans, maize, cocoyams, cassava, yams, vegetables, and plantains, or gathered firewood. In the rainy season, it would sometimes rain all day, and we'd be pestered by intermittent rain showers followed by breaks of sunshine and then more rain. Once we got home, everyone had to clean up, and once she put the pot of food on the fire, she'd begin mundane conversations that more often than not seemed to end up with *ble.* She had ten hungry mouths to feed, and what better way to keep her children from fidgeting, crying, complaining than to keep them active, involve them in lively sessions of riddling and storytelling? I am not suggesting that my mother did this every day; however, there is no doubt that she used storytelling, before and after meals, to instruct, to mother, to maintain a sense of family and cohesion. She often got us to do chores as a group with the same ruse. On the evenings when palm wine was being consumed after the meal, she'd goad the children into testing their wits with riddles and then quietly haul out to the parlor the basin(s) of groundnuts, maize, or *egusi* that she wanted shelled. While we worked, she would weave baskets or mend one thing or another.

It is this gendered, multidimensional function of *ble* that I am trying to capture here. The riddle sessions always did the trick. You got interested in the riddles, you showed off how much you knew or had learned, you fought over answers, and you were hooked. Once hooked, you couldn't fall asleep or immediately leave. Riddles are therefore the corncob a child roasts and nibbles on to appease the growl in his/her stomach while the evening meal cooks. Riddles are the anthills standing between a boy and the tree at which he aims the arc of his urine. Riddles are the call-response drumbeat baiting the participants to hours of evening activity, relaxation, and *ble*. Like the downpour soaking a termite-filled anthill on a starlit dry-season night, riddles are the revivifying petrichor luring *ble* out of their groves.

Le (lend me your ears), the riddler shouts.
Nkwang (we are listening), the audience responds.
"I build my house with one stick."
"A mushroom."

Le
Nkwang
"I build my house without a door."
"An egg."

Le
Nkwang
"I visit everyone but no one can visit me."
"The eye."

Le
Nkwang
"I eat all I want but I am never full."
"The earth."

Le
Nkwang
"I am a house with no walls."
"You are the sky."

Le
Nkwang
"I eat with my mouth and I shit with my mouth."
"A bat."

Le
Nkwang
"Little stones on a scarp face."
"Breasts."

Le
Nkwang
"Little stones in a net."
"Testicles."

Le
Nkwang
"A small stone with many sides."
"A cashew nut."

Le
Nkwang
"Running water on a scarp face."
"Tears."
"Catarrh."

Le
Nkwang
"That which touches or knocks on the head of the fon and the head of the commoner."
"A razor."
"Death."

Le
Nkwang
"That which does not revere a fon."
"A razor."
"Death."
"Illness."
"Rain."
"A jigger."

Le
Nkwang
"Standing on top of a hill calling for its death."
"A cricket."
"Grains of paradise."
"Alligator pepper."

Le
Nkwang
"My house has no lamp."
"You are a grave."

Le
Nkwang
"When I am young I refuse to lie down when asked; when I am old I refuse to stand up when asked. What am I?"
"You are breasts."

Le
Nkwang
"That which goes on a journey and never returns."
"The river."
"A gunshot."

Le
Nkwang
"I am invisible."
"You are a fart."
"You are the wind."

Le
Nkwang
"A soldier standing on top of the hill with his fangs exposed."
"A steel trap."

Le
Nkwang
"Silver giants with long, spindly legs."
"Rain."

Le
Nkwang
"An old woman with exposed genitalia."
"A raffia tree at the end of the tapping cycle."

Le
Nkwang
"If I am not circumcised I cannot urinate."
"You are a calabash."

Le
Nkwang
"I am black when I am young and red when I am old."
"Palm nuts."

Le
Nkwang
"When I am young, I wear *atante;* my skin is red; when I am middle-aged I am pink, and in my old age I wear *ndip;* the sheen of my skin is black. What am I?"
"You are a plum."

Le
Nkwang
"I never sleep."
"A waterfall."

Le
Nkwang
"I am a fish in a pool of water surrounded by warriors carrying spears."

"The answer is the tongue in your mouth surrounded by teeth."

Le
Nkwang
"I am a stream with many crabs and one fish."
"You are the mouth."

Le
Nkwang
"At dawn I walk with four legs, at noon I walk with two legs, at dusk I walk with three legs. What am I?"
"You are a human being."

Notes

1. Mount Cameroon erupted in 1909, 1922, 1954, 1959, 1982, 1999, and 2000. There were a similar number of eruptions in the nineteenth century. See http://www.bakwerilands.org/fako.htm. Popular superstition holds that the mountain erupts when the god that sustains it is angry and its fury can only be appeased with the sacrifice of an albino. Stories about Mount Cameroon transcend the national popular imagination. The Victorian Englishwoman Mary Kingsley (of *Travels in West Africa* fame), for one, wrote a fascinating account,"Ascent of the Great Peak of Cameroons," of her experience in 1895. Similarly, the Mount Cameroon Race is an international competition held annually in which runners race to the summit and down the slopes of the mountain. The race began in the 1970s and is now a popular attraction for tourists and runners from around the world.

2. For a detailed discussion of the peoples of Cameroon before European incursions, see Tambi Eyongetah Mbuagbaw, Robert Brain, and Robin Palmer's *A History of the Cameroon*, 2nd ed. (Essex: Longman, 1987), 1–41.

3. Duala people are known to comment that *mbea towè* are so plentiful in the estuary in the rainy season, especially in August, that the poor can then afford to eat prawns. This observation is grounded

in local complaints that since prawns became an important export item, Cameroonians have access only to puny shrimp while the big juicy ones are exported to European markets that pay prices locals cannot afford.

4. The struggle for self-determination and independence for "The Southern Cameroons" was officially launched with the April 1993 All Anglophone Conference (AAC) in Buea, followed by the second AAC conference in Bamenda in April/May 1994. The AAC has since been renamed the Southern Cameroons Peoples Conference (SCPC) and, later yet, the Southern Cameroons Peoples Organisation (SCAPO) and is regarded as the umbrella organization for the struggle. Prominent groups include the Cameroon Anglophone Movement (CAM); Ambazonia; Free West Cameroon Movement; and the Southern Cameroons Youth League.

5. In 1961, UNESCO and the French government collaborated in creating the National Institute for University Studies, which became the Federal University of Cameroon in 1962 and later the Université de Yaoundé (University of Yaounde). Professional or specialized programs of higher learning such as IRIC (International Relations Institute of Cameroon), CUSS (Centre Universitaire des Sciences de la Santé—School of Medicine), ENAM (École Normale d'Administration et de Magistrature—School of Administration and Magistracy), ENS (École Normale Supérieure—School of Education), ENSP (École Normale Supérieure Polytechnique—School of Engineering), EMIA (École Militaire Inter-Armes—School of Armed Forces), ENJS (École Nationale de Jeunesse et des Sports—National School of Youth and Sports), and ESIJY (École Supérieure Internationale de Journalisme de Yaoundé—International School of Journalism) were created in the late 1960s and early 1970s and coexisted with the University of Yaounde. Five university satellite centers were also created, each catering to one specialty, for instance, agriculture, agronomy, and so on. These centers were made into full-fledged universities in 1998: University of Yaounde II (the former University of Yaounde was renamed University of Yaounde I), University of Douala, University of Buea (touted as Anglo-Saxon oriented), University of Dschang, and University of Ngaoundere.

6. Cameroon's population is today estimated at about fifteen million people.

7. Diana C. Newton, "Autonomous Publishing in Cameroon," in the *African Book Publishing Record* 17, no. 2 (1991): 95–99. See also

Karen R. Keim, "Popular Fiction Publishing in Cameroon," in *African Book Publishing Record* 9, no. 1 (1983): 7–11.

8. Newton, "Autonomous Publishing," 96.

9. Many collections of oral narratives by francophone Cameroon authors such as Léon-Marie Ayissi (1968), Isaac Tchoumba Ngouankeu (1969), Joseph Marie Awouma (1976, 1978, 1979), Jourdain Innocent Noah (1976, 1978), Charles Binam Bikoi (1978), Emmanuel Soundjock (1978), D. Beling-Nkoumba (1978, 1981, 1983, 1985), and M. Le Lievre (1983) were published during this period of cultural rejuvenation and celebration by Éditions CLÉ and only later by CEPMAE/CEPER and SOPECAM.

10. See, for instance, Ambe Suh Achuo, "Folktales from Bafut" (1975); Bernard Ndofor Tangey, "A Literary Research on Bambili (Mbeligi) Folktales" (1975); Joseph Kum Mua, "Aghem Oral Literature: A General Survey" (1979); Alembong Nol, "Divine Images in Nweh Oral Literature" (1981); Paul Mbangwana, "Cameroon Oral Tales in Ngemba" (1983); and Juliana Makuchi Nfah, "The Image of the Woman in Beba Folktales" (1981) and "A Literary Analysis of the Folktale among the Beba" (1987), to name a few. The glaring disparity meant a dearth of published collections in English: Daniel Lantum's *Folk Tales of Nso'*, originally published by the Nso History Society in 1964, republished as *Tales of Nso* (Lagos: African Universities Press, 1969); Loreto Todd and Geoffrey Whittam, *Tortoise the Trickster and Other Folktales from Cameroon* (New York: Schocken Books, 1979); *Folktales of Cameroon* (Yaounde: American Cultural Center, 1974). Some folktales are included in Tala Kashim's self-published *An Introduction to Cameroon Oral Literature*, printed by SOPECAM (1984); Comfort Ashu, Adrew Kemba Mosongo, and Oumarou S Mohmbawarr, *Riddles and Folktales for Schools* (Limbe, Cameroon: Nooremac Press, 1984); Jonas Ndah's self-published *Around the Fire: African Stories for Children* (Buea, 1988); Emmanuel Matateyou, *An Anthology of Myths, Legends, and Folktales from Cameroon* (Lewiston, NY: Edwin Mellen Press, 1997); Patrick Mbunwe-Samba's self-published *Wimbum Ancestral Voices: Cameroon Folktale Heritage* (1993) and *Shadows in the Firelight: A Selection of Cameroon Folktales* (Bamenda, 1998).

11. Cameroon is made up of ten administrative units known as provinces, each headed by a governor: Adamawa, Central, East, Extreme North, Littoral, North, North West, South, South West, and West.

12. It must be noted that such geographical entities reflect colonial boundaries that paid little heed to the cultural and/or political synergies

of the groups of people being lumped together. They continued to serve as convenient administrative units in the post-colonial context.

13. See "The Beba-Befang Clan" and "Cameroon—Administrative" maps.

14. In 1993, Menchum Valley Subdivision with its headquarters at Benakuma was created; Beba-Befang, along with villages of the "Essimbi Clan," now fall under this administrative unit.

15. Complicating this is the fact that Beba borders Momo, Mezam, and Menchum divisions. Bafut, located in Mezam Division, is laying claim to some Beba territory. Boundary disputes are therefore fueling the drive to remap Menchum borders and consequently, Beba boundaries.

16. In 1983, sociolinguists working on the Linguistic Atlas of Cameroon classified Beba as a dialect of Bafut (*Atlas Linguistique de l'Afrique Centrale [ALAC] / Atlas Linguistique du Cameroun [ALCAM]* [Paris: Agence de coopération culturelle et technique; Yaoundé, Cameroun: Centre régional de recherche et de documentation sur les traditions orales et pour le développement des langues africaines, 1983], 401). In 2000, Grimes also listed Beba and Bombe villages as speaking a dialect of Bafut. However, after their 2001 SIL/Ministry of Scientific and Technical Research study in Beba and Bombe, "Rapid Appraisal Sociolinguistic Survey of Beba [ALCAM 912]," Brye et al. concluded that Beba is not a dialect of Bafut and should be entered as its own language and assigned its own ALCAM number.

17. Bombe is mentioned in the story "Penis, Testicles, and Vagina." I am grateful to Mama Monica Agha for this paragraph on Agha Nefo and the succession disputes that followed his disappearance.

18. *Bo,* plural, meaning children of (singular, *mo*), as in Bo Adieh Yiboh—children of Adieh Yiboh; Bodo—children of Adoh; *ba* and *be,* meaning people of.

19. The *Batolah* are sometimes contemptuously referred to as being endogamous.

20. Plural, *bejindia*; singular, *njindia*—literally, he who has eaten or won the house of; therefore, heir to the house of.

21. Rural exodus began with the men who in colonial times traveled "down south," to the South West Province, that is, to work in German plantations—rubber, palm, banana, and so on. With time, the men returned home and got married or took other male relatives with them to work in these plantations (the British later took over the plantations from the Germans). As a result, the population of Beba

people in the South West grew. Today, many Beba still work in the plantations now known as the Cameroon Development Corporation (CDC). However, the benefits of education and concomitant jobs in other urban areas, coupled with modern trade, have changed the face and direction of rural exodus from that of fifty years ago.

22. *Nki Mbu*, or River Mbu, is an important river in Beba.

23. See for instance, Vladimir Propp, "The Tale as a Whole," in *Morphology of the Folktale* (Austin: University of Texas Press, 1968), 92–117; William Bascom, "The Forms of Folklore: Prose Narratives," *Journal of American Folklore* 78, no. 307 (January–March 1965): 3–20; Ruth H. Finnegan, "Prose Narratives," in *Oral Literature in Africa* (Oxford: Oxford University Press, 1970), 315–88; Denise Paulme, "Morphologie du conte africain," in *La mère dévorante: Essai sur la morphologie des contes africains* (Paris: Gallimard, 1976), 19–50; Isidore Okpewho, "Oral Narratives," in *African Oral Literature: Backgrounds, Character, and Continuity* (Bloomington: Indiana University Press, 1992), 163–225; Donald Cosentino, "African Oral Narrative Traditions," in *Teaching Oral Traditions*, ed. John Miles Foley (New York: Modern Language Association, 1998), 174–88. In his book, Okpewho incisively analyzes previous debates in the field while clarifying as well as moving beyond the lapses and/or problematic positions advanced by previous scholars of African oral literature.

24. Even today, I remember the hauntingly sad tone of my mother's narration, especially when she sang the song.

25. The presentation of the folktales in parts 1, 2, and 3 was done for convenience. In my retelling, I simply stuck with the pattern we followed when we told *ble* at home.

26. Storytellers can make choices that historically situate them in or distance them from the stories they tell; for example, use of the German mark, the British pound, or the CFA franc lends specific historical meanings in a Cameroonian context. In the story "The Boy and the Dish," I chose to use "dish" although some older family members who tell this story use "calabash bowl" instead. However, for a more concise literary effect, I preferred "*awawa* leaves," even though I could have used the modern counterpart known as the "iron sponge." One can thus choose to adapt idioms to suit one's own telling and for specific effect.

27. *Beh*, meaning people; *kop*, meaning secret society; a specialized, select, or distinguished group.